FLY COUNTRY

A Golden Age Murder Mystery

Anthony Lang

Spitfire Publishers

CONTENTS

ABOUT 'FLY COUNTRY'

A man is discovered shot though the head in a London bedsit. A revolver lies nearby and personal papers burned in the grate. The dead man's involvement in the sale of an African copper mine concession appears unrelated. Patricia Repton, the young City financier who brokered the deal, is suspicious; as is the widow of the mining engineer who discovered the valuable metal deposit. The engineer had recently met with a gruesome death in the African bush when his .577 large calibre hunting rifle misfired on a stampeding buffalo. Patricia joins forces with Scotland Yard's Detective-Inspector Hoe to investigate, uncovering maleficence, multiple murder and fraud.

About the Author

Anthony Lang was one of no less than *nine* pseudonyms adopted by Anglo-Irish detective fiction author, Jack Vahey. Born John George Hazlette Vahey in Belfast in 1881 he worked first as an apprentice architect, then an accountant before finally turning to writing fiction full-time. He is perhaps best known by his 'Vernon Loder' pseudonym used on twenty-two of his novels, many published in the prestigious Collins Crime Club, the first *The Mystery at Stowe* in 1928, the last, *Kill in the Ring*, in 1938. Jack Vahey died in 1938.

Praise for the Author

'Effortless telling of a good story and meticulous observation of the rules'
The Observer

'Character drawing in Vernon Loder's strong point'
Glasgow Herald

'A master story-teller'
Manchester Evening News

'The name of Mr Loder must be widely known as a reliable and promising indication on the cover of a detective story'
Times Literary Supplement

'One of the most promising recruits to the ranks of detective story writers'
F.T. Smith, Collins Crime Club Editor

Writing as Anthony Lang

Fly Country
'A neatly constructed plot which is distinctly out of the ordinary'
The Times
'An excellent mystery story... it is told extremely well'
Liverpool Post
'A clever plot'
Irish Independent
'A murder mystery story... an original plot'
Sheffield Independent

The Crime
'A brilliantly-written detective story... has an unexpected climax'
The Daily Mail
'Holds the readers in suspense to almost the last page... a capital yarn'
Dundee Advertiser
'Ingenious'

Aberdeen Press & Journal
'A detective story of the first order'
Cassell's Weekly

Writing as George Varney

The Missing Link
'Detective mystery in a sinister old mansion'
Daily Sketch
'Varney's tale of detection has an unusual merit'
Morning Post
'Exciting'
The Spectator

Writing as Vernon Loder

The Mystery at Stowe
'An ingenious problem and an ingenious solution... can be warmly recommended'
The Observer
'A very pretty and ingenious mystery'
Times Literary Supplement
'A well-written and skilfully constructed story'
Nigel Moss

The Shop Window Murder
'A decidedly ingenious story'
Times Literary Supplement
'A stroke of genius'
Daily Herald

Between Twelve and One
'A murder most ingeniously contrived'
New York Times
'A brilliant bit of investigating and deduction by Superintendent Cobham solves the apparently impenetrable mystery'
The Bookman

The Death Pool

'Vernon Loder spins out his gruesome tale and does it well'
New York Times

CHAPTER 1 PATRICIA STARTS WORK

Patricia Repton's office was a very businesslike place, though, so far, business itself was noticeably lacking.

In the outer office sat Miss Froud, an unimaginative but quick typist. She sat at a stiff typing table, and to every side of her stood the latest appliances in modern business furniture, from the latest thing in filing cabinets, to a dictaphone; with steel cupboards which positively gaped for lack of papers and documents.

The second room was dedicated to Patricia herself, and was only less severe in that it boasted a little Wilton carpet, a roll-top desk, and a vase of fresh flowers. The rest of the furniture was a match for that in the outer room in its suggestion of efficient modernity.

Patricia had taken an Honours degree at Girham, and this furniture might have helped to convince the sceptical that the pretty girl with the shingled hair full of warm lights, with brown eyes that always smiled, and a mouth that enmeshed mirth in its upturned corners, was really not only a woman of looks but of books.

To most people a mathematical scholar should have a face and figure made of Euclid's favourite angles!

This morning she was sitting at her desk, smiling bewitchingly at an elderly beau who had deposited himself nicely in the client's arm-chair. He was, however, so much in earnest that he appeared to ignore the delectable experience of basking in Patricia's smile.

A white-haired man of between sixty and seventy, he betrayed signs of careful valeting. His face was fine-drawn, delicate of feature. His single eyeglass, unrimmed, was held at this moment between his white, tapered fingers, and he surveyed the girl as if looking for some speck the vulgar life of the city might have deposited on her.

"Why not marriage?" he said suddenly, with the air of a man making a discovery.

He screwed the monocle into his eye, and waited to hear the effect of his pronouncement. Patricia smiled still.

"Isn't this rather sudden, Mr Elphinstone?"

He had been born without a sense of humour, and shook his head. "It's a solution, my dear Patricia."

"As if I were a cross-word puzzle!" she laughed.

He raised his eyebrows. His newspaper did not boast such things.

"A solution for your problem. You must see it—must understand that your father's daughter is as out of place here as ——"

"As an ignoramus among the knowing," she suggested. "No, I don't see that. It doesn't trouble me. What does trouble me is feeling like a hungry spider in my web here, with no flies to catch!"

He shivered at the unsavoury simile. "I am really alarmed for you, Patricia. You are—what? A broker? A financial agent?"

"Betwixt and between."

"Very well. Jane and I offer you the shelter of our home. No, don't thank me again, my dear! You have refused, so there is an end to it. What I mean is this. I was startled and worried a year ago when I heard that your poor father's affairs had been left in such a tangle. I hear—I trust I was misinformed—that he left you a bare thousand pounds."

"Of which this office and its furniture devoured six hundred," she agreed.

6

"Dear me! Dear me! And how do you propose to live on four hundred?"

She laughed. "I don't! I hope the business will keep me."

He shook his head sadly. "My life has not been passed in commercial circles. I am sorry to say that I know no one whom I could throw in your way. Marriage is another matter. Think it over, Patricia. Jane and I agree that it is best."

"My love to her," said Patricia smiling, as he rose. "If you consider it, Mr Elphinstone, marriage requires two people to think it over. I don't know that I am really in favour of Leap Year."

He held out his hand. "Well, I hope you will be prosperous, and safe. I wonder. As I came along the street, I noticed the sad lack of manners. Jostling, hurrying, no rest! But I am not so young as I was, and little things worry me. Goodbye, my dear."

"A dear old thing, but how alarming!" Patricia said to herself, when she had shown him out. "The City seems to him a rodeo and an American crook-film all in one."

She went into the outer office. Miss Froud returned a tiny mirror to a tiny bag and sat up, brightening a little under the influence of her employer's beaming face.

"You must be rather bored," said Patricia. "If this goes on much longer, I must write letters to myself."

"Are you going to advertise again, Miss Repton?"

"No. The last time I had three reporters, eighteen canvassers, two charitable appeals, and the agent of a society for inducing women to eliminate men."

"Cranks," said Miss Froud, sniffing.

"I think, instead, of writing a letter to the papers about women in business," said Patricia. "They always seem to write in a grumbling tone. I shall try the other tack. Now, that will be something nice for you to do. I shall sit down to the dictaphone at once, and when I have done you shall copy it out a dozen times. You might type the addresses of twelve London and provincial papers now. It's a low trick, but business is low with us."

Miss Froud smiled. "I don't see it is."

"Do you mean the state of our business or the letter?" asked Patricia?" Never mind! We may snare someone."

She returned to her room, lit a cigarette, and thought over the terms of the letter.

Miss Froud appeared five minutes later. She looked excited and almost moved as she closed the communicating door behind her.

"It's a client!" she whispered eagerly. "Mr Hanaper, he calls himself. Can he see you?"

Patricia smiled. "Quick! Lock the door behind him, and see that he doesn't escape!"

Miss Froud, in spite of her unimaginativeness, was keenly interested in Patricia's venture. She smiled, and went out again, to usher in the client.

Mr Hanaper's appearance did a good deal to dissipate Patricia's hopes. He was a man of middle height, with a ragged brown beard, deep-set blue eyes, and a tweed suit cut so square in the shoulders, and so baggy everywhere that, in combination with the "smasher" hat he carried in his hand, he appeared to be a visitant from the back of beyond.

"Sit down, please," she said, as Miss Froud closed the door. "Will you smoke?"

He looked at the box of cigarettes she pushed towards him, but hesitated before he took one. "Thank you, miss," he said.

His voice was rough and uncultured, and she noticed that the hand which selected the cigarette was broad, coarse, wrinkled and sunburnt, with spatulate fingers.

He had had a little attaché-case in one hand, and it was now across his knee. He lighted up, holding a cupped palm round the match, as if used to open spaces, and Patricia wondered if he were a prospector from abroad.

"I understood that you wanted to see me on business?" she said.

"Yes, miss," he replied, opening the case and extracting a bundle of stained and crumpled papers, "and a dismal business it's been, I can tell you. Seems to me they take every one for a liar in this place."

"Then yours must be a mining proposition," said she, with a twinkle.

He nodded. "That's what it is, miss, and rich, too. Why, it'd make these Katanga mines look like tuppence."

"Then it's African?"

"It is, miss. I found it myself, and I spent all I had on getting expert advice. Tom Gores went over it, and he was AMICE and other names that mean he knew metals and things like that from A to Z. Best pal I ever had was Tom, until he did a fool trick following up a wounded buffalo in bush and got snuffed out."

"The trouble is that there are quite a few experts who give optimistic reports," said Patricia, looking at him. "The City commonly uses the large end of the telescope. Have you tried this elsewhere?"

"Have I tried it elsewhere!" The phrase in his mouth was not mocking, but bitter and wearied. "Why, miss, I've been with a score of big men, and they either laughed at it, or wanted to buy me out for two or three thousand pound. I'm not having any!"

"Are those the papers connected with it?" asked Patricia.

"All of them, miss. When I was passing this block I see your name on the board as financial agent. That's what I want, finance."

"Have you a list of all your documents?"

He fished for a paper and handed it over. Patricia glanced at it. "Do you mind if my typist takes a copy of this? You see, I should have to look into it carefully, and that will take time. I should, of course, give you a receipt for the papers."

"Of course, miss. But, look here, I want ten thousand down and ten per cent, on the take when the proposition gets going."

"I do not act direct," she said.

"I know that, miss. But I want to tell you the terms so you can put them before people. Them's my lowest."

Patricia rang a bell which was answered by Miss Froud.

"Take copies of this list," she said. "Let me have it as soon as you can."

Miss Froud took the list, glanced furtively at the bearded man, and returned to her office. Hanaper crushed out his cigarette end on the ash-tray.

"Do you think there is any hope, miss?"

Patricia thought him rather pathetic. "Well, I can't give an opinion yet. But you may rely on me if I think there is something in it, Mr Hanaper. I am quite aware that slips have been made in the City before now, and opportunities thrown away. Will you let me have your address? Then if you call about this time tomorrow, I will be able to go into the matter more thoroughly."

She passed him a sheet of paper and her fountain pen, and he carefully wrote his name, and an address in Willesden.

"I charge the usual fees."

He looked at her awkwardly, and she hastened to add, "But only if business is done."

"Right, miss," he said. "Some of them wanted me to hand money over first. I haven't got it. I put my all in this; my life too! The Belgies would have done me in if they could, and the Portuguese, too. Wanted to make out it was over the border."

Miss Froud came in with the list and the copy. Patricia handed the original to Hanaper, and read over the copy quickly. He agreed with it, signed the copy, and received a receipt for the documents he had brought with him.

Then he got up. "Well, miss, I'm sure I'm much obliged to you," he said, holding out his hand. "It'll be a great day for me if you can sell for me."

"We'll do our best," said Patricia, smiling. "Tomorrow, then, at this time."

When he had gone, she sat down to go through the documents. First she read them through carefully, then she studied the rough maps and surveys, then she went back to certain documents, and read them again more carefully.

So far as the actual concession was concerned, everything appeared to be in order. A native chief, acting under the advice of a British assistant commissioner, had granted the concession. A mining expert, Mr Thomas Gores, had reported on the area after survey in the most favourable terms. It was true there was no railhead near, to promise transportation of the most economical kind, but there was a river, and Mr Gores had reported that there was a prospect of securing cheap labour on the spot.

"Now what is the snag, I wonder?" she asked herself, as she sat back in her chair after two hours devoted to the documents. "Every prospect pleases and only the City man refuses to believe it! I wonder if Mr Thomas Gores was a truthful person as well as a good pal?"

It was after her usual lunch time, so she locked up the papers in a steel safe, told Miss Froud she would not be more than three-quarters of an hour, and went off to the Guildhall Library.

There, in a book of reference, she came on the name of Mr T Gores.

He had half the engineering alphabet after his name, and his credentials were impeccable. She noticed that he had been consulting engineer to the African Cobus Co, and rang them up when she left the library. Then she went to lunch, having been assured that Mr Gores was actually dead, had paid the price paid too often by keen but over-reckless hunters, and was buried somewhere near Kilima N'jaro.

"All clear, so far," she mused as she ate. "I must look into those papers again."

When she returned to the office she sent Miss Froud out for her lunch, and sat down again to study Mr Hanaper's documents; this time with a minuteness that presently justified itself. She came across a note on the corner of a paper, almost rubbed out. Evidently it had been written in pencil by one of the financial people to whom the proposition had been submitted. It ran thus:

"Hanaper's yarn won't wash. This is Belgian territory, and no mistake.—E de V."

Patricia carefully completed the erasing. "So that is it! I wonder if Mr E de V is sure of his ground? Poor Mr Hanaper evidently left that for all to see."

She left her desk to get a directory, and there, after half an hour, she discovered a Mr Eduard de Villegaile, agent for the Cie Carasta Anonyme.

"Cher Eduard may be after the thing himself," she mused. "I want to know more about that."

Her mind circled over the names of her friends, and settled on one young man who was in the Foreign Office. She rang him up promptly and put a question. He promised a reply in an hour, and she accepted an invitation to a play with him, and rang off. When Miss Froud came back, she felt that she had not made a bad start.

"Do you think there is anything in it?" asked Miss Froud, anxiously, "Or not?"

"There may be," said Patricia. "Even if there is, I may have some trouble getting someone to look into it seriously. But the great thing after all is to make a beginning."

Her friend at the Foreign Office was better than his word. In half an hour he rang up.

"That forsaken spot you were asking after, old thing," he began conversationally, "is certainly not in the territory of Belgium. The boundary commission years ago made it ten miles our side. That was confirmed in the treaty. But what particular busy bee is tormenting your bonnet? Are you turning slave-trader, or something?"

"I'm thinking of it," said Patricia. "Awfully good of you anyway to put me on. But I haven't any time for badinage now. I'm frightfully busy. Got a client, you know."

"Good egg!" said the voice. "Grapple him to you with hooks of steel, old thing!—So long."

"And that's that!" said Patricia with satisfaction, as she put down the receiver. "Mon cher Eduard is a trifle off the line."

CHAPTER 2 A SECOND CLIENT

Before Patricia left the office that evening, she had drawn up a guarded advertisement with regard to the copper proposition, and Miss Froud, glad of an opportunity to do something, had taken it round to three newspapers.

While she was away, Patricia rang up the London office of the African company represented by Mr Eduard de Villegaile. Here she was taking advantage of her femininity, and trusting to the chivalry of the Belgian to answer some enquiries he might not have accorded attention had she been an unknown man.

She got through to him after a short conversation with one of his clerks, apologising for encroaching on his time, and adding that women new to business must rely on their male confréres for initiation.

"Madame flatters me," said a smooth voice, with hardly a trace of foreign accent. "May I felicitate madame on her entry into a profession rarely adopted by her charming sex?"

"Milles remerciments," said Patricia, laughing. "But, monsieur, one fears that one day felicitations may give place to reproaches!"

"Impossible!" was the gallant reply, "But I am quite at madame's service."

"Thank you, monsieur, you are most kind. I understand that you are one of the foremost experts on Africa, and a proposition has just been put before me with regard to a concession at

Bangele. Is it not in the territory of your government?"

He replied at once, and his smooth voice betrayed nothing, "Bangele? One refreshes one's memory, madame.—A moment. —No. I can assure you that you are mistaken. It is, one understands, near our border, but not of it."

"You are certain of that?"

"But absolutely. There was a commission—some claim once. But it was decided against us. Rest assured, madame, that you may safely proceed on the assumption that it remains within your own powerful empire."

Patricia bit her lip, "By the way, monsieur," she said, "I suppose your company does not consider propositions outside your own territory."

"Au contraire," he said, "we are always happy to consider definite business anywhere."

"Then perhaps this has been put before you already?" said she. "The name of my client is Hanaper—HANAPER."

The Belgian again replied at once, "No, madame. We have not seen it here. I do not know the name."

There was a pause, then Patricia resumed in a coaxing tone, "It is an impertinence on my part, perhaps, monsieur, but I wonder if you would let me have a little note stating that Bangele is in British territory."

"If it is the Bangele which stands *vis à vis* Guala I shall have pleasure in meeting madame's wishes," said he. "But why does not madame call?"

"I shall be happy to do so," said Patricia. "I might, with my client's permission, lay the matter before you. In the meantime your pronouncement on this place and its situation will be valuable to me."

"I am happy to have been of assistance even the most minute," he replied.

"Now who is the liar?" Patricia mused, when she at last rang off: "the half-erased note, or M Eduard? Or are the initials 'E de V' those of some other man?"

She went home to her little flat, still wondering, and while she cooked a sole in the tiny kitchenette attached to it, she came to the conclusion that she had made a mistake. If M de Villegaile had already considered the copper proposition, he would either have said so at once, or informed her that the affair did not interest him. That the writer of the annotation was a Belgian she still firmly believed, but it was not the polite foreigner who had answered her questions that afternoon.

Dick Caley, who was in the Foreign Office, called for her later, and took her to the theatre. While they were in the taxi, he put an amused question.

"When do you take your ticket for Bangele, Pat? I know you are a swell at maths, but I didn't know you were going to take up research."

"Don't be an ass, Dick," she begged him. "What's the matter with Bangele?"

"Flies," said he, grinning. "There are flies on Bangele."

"You're sure it's not bats in the belfry?"

"Yours, if you go there, certainly, old thing. It's fly country —tse-tse, *gloxina palpalis*—sleeping-sickness, and that sort of thing, on the wing.—Now do you get me?"

"Of course," she said, staring. "But is that true? You're not trying to be funny?"

"The Foreign Office is never funny," he replied. "Curious and quaint at times, but never funny. With us the joker has no career. He is kaput from the start."

"Then it is in the fly belt?"

"I said so. They're talking of sending out a little expedition of experts on tropical diseases.—Don't go!"

"I hadn't thought of it. It is a business affair," she said, thoughtfully.

"Oh, that's another pair of sleeves," he returned. "But here is our show. If you can turn your overburdened mind from business for a couple of hours, I may not repent a wasted guinea."

As Patricia fell asleep that night, she wondered if M de Villegaile would write. When she reached the office the next morning, she found that he had been as good as his word.

The letter was typed, of course, but at the foot of it, he had written his name in a small and beautiful hand. Patricia sat up, literally and figuratively, when she looked at it. Her visual memory was excellent, and she had not the least doubt that the capital letters of M de Villegaile's name were those which had figured as initials on Mr Hanaper's document.

"Great Scott!" said Patricia. "What a nasty little man! Lying to a lady too! I have a good mind not to call on him after all."

Three folded newspapers lay on her desk. She opened them in turn and found her advertisement adequately displayed. Then she saw Miss Froud, told her to show in Mr Hanaper the moment he arrived, and betook herself anew to a study of the documents in connection with the copper proposition.

She was not one of those complacent women who conclude that a university education fits them at once to handle any business, however complicated or unfamiliar, but she did conclude now that she could see no obvious flaw in Hanaper's documents. Dick Caley had perhaps put his finger unknowingly on the weak spot. If the district was devastated by sleeping-sickness, it would be even more difficult to recruit native labour than to secure a European staff to exploit the concession.

But why had de Villegaile first considered the proposition, turned it down on a false excuse, then lied to her and professed to know nothing of Mr Hanaper? She was still worrying over this, wondering if her first client would after all turn out to be an unprofitable one, when Mr Hanaper himself was shown in.

He exhibited the same signs of hesitancy, and modest clumsiness which had characterised him the day before. But he sat down, and took a cigarette, while she outlined what she had already done—omitting her visit to the Guildhall Library, and her telephone call to de Villegaile.

"But now there is a real Negro in the fence," she said, her eyes fixed on his—"a nasty Negro, too, who may put his black foot out to trip us. Sleeping-sickness is his name, Mr Hanaper."

Hanaper did not blink. He smiled a little.

"Well, miss, it does just show you what stale news they have here at home about Africa. Fifteen years ago there was a scare about Bangele and fly. I was there at the time, and I scooted proper fast, I can tell you. I have had my whack of malaria and some other diseases, but I admit I fight shy of sleeping-sickness, as every man does who has seen it."

"You mean that the country is clear of it now?"

"I mean that, for some reason or other, no fly has made its appearance within two hundred miles of it, anyway up to last March. I was there then. unless yours is later news."

"I don't think it is," said Patricia. "By the way, do you mind if I put this before the Belgian Carasta people?"

He shook his head, "No use, miss. They turned it down."

"Oh, did they?" she glanced at him. "Well, Mr Hanaper, I have already advertised the thing, and I am ready to try to negotiate your proposition. That is all I can say today, but it I have any enquiries of a likely kind I shall at once communicate with you."

"No one been in about it yet, miss?" he enquired as he got up.

Patricia, laughed lightly. "Business doesn't move as fast as that here, Mr Hanaper. I suppose it's our heavier climate. But you may rely on my doing my best."

"If he'd denied letting the Carasta people see it, I would have known he was the liar, not my polite Belgian friend," said Patricia to herself, when he had gone. "As it is, I must keep my eye on E de V. He seems to me what the vulgar call a twister."

She had three calls that day with regard to the concession. It had become known that a charming young woman had set up as a financial agent, and curiosity more than copper directed the callers to her office. But all three discovered that a charming young woman can be very freezing on occasion, and the fat old man who came last positively suffered from frostbite when he emerged from the office and made hastily for the lift. But then he was a famous Silenus, and his leer would have alarmed a stone Venus. Patricia went home that evening wondering if the financial thickets were regularly sanctuaries for satyrs.

As she went down again to the city the following morning,

the precise and delicate figure of Mr Elphinstone did arise once or twice before her mental eye. He had made her a charming offer. He was her father's old friend. At his house she would meet the people she knew. On one side was hospitality and a familiar milieu, on the other a losing battle with strange antagonists and no allies.

Then her lips set firm. "I am not going to freeze out before I get into the game," she said to herself. "Dear old dad would have detested a daughter with cold feet."

Miss Froud was still killing time with an effort when she arrived. She herself had not the heart to get out those documents again and consider them. Almost she knew them by heart. Instead, she sat down with a financial directory, and began to make out a list of people to whom the proposition might be shown.

At eleven she gave the list to be typed; at five minutes past Miss Froud announced a fresh caller.

"Is he fat and red of face," asked Patricia, "does he grin like a Cheshire cat, and smile like an overripe Stilton? If he does, tell him I'm busy."

Miss Froud shook her head vigorously. "He's quite young, Miss Repton, and good-looking. His name is Peter Carey. Will you see him?"

"Did he mention his business?"

Miss Froud nodded. "He had the paper in his hand, with the advertisement."

"Probably he is a clerk from some firm," said Patricia. "Show him in, please."

That this last conjecture was a mistake the appearance of Mr Carey at once attested. He appeared to be about twenty-five, a slim young man, though well-muscled about the shoulders, with a quiet but attractive face, to which two serious grey eyes gave a thoughtful look. But his mouth had pleasant lines, and his walk was that of a man who is shy but not ill-at-ease. Her first glance at his clothes told her that here was no subordinate in a city office unable to afford the luxury of an expert tailor.

He looked at Patricia with an air of surprise which was not impertinent. Evidently he had not guessed at the possibility that a financial agent could be a woman of youth and charm.

"I come to see you about this advertisement," he said, when he had bowed to Patricia. "The African concession, you know."

"Good," said Patricia. "Sit down, Mr Carey. The business only came into my hands two days ago, and I have not been able to go into it yet as thoroughly as I could wish. But I may tell you at once that it is a copper-mining proposition not yet developed, and the initial expenditure will be high."

He sat down. "I didn't expect to get it for nothing, of course. If I satisfy myself that it is worth while, that can be arranged."

"Money!" said Patricia to herself, and added aloud, "At present it is in the air. There is the concession. That is valid enough. There is a report from a well-known mining engineer as to the potentialities of the area. He speaks of the possibilities in the highest terms. But perhaps you are interested in copper, and know a great deal more about it than I do."

He smiled suddenly and became less stiff: "Indeed, I don't. The fact is, Miss Repton, that I have just inherited a good deal of money, and I want to go abroad. I thought I should like to have an interest in something that would take me out there."

His naturalness interested her. "Don't you think in that case it would be better to get your solicitor to represent you?"

He shook his head. "There's been too much of that in our family, Miss Repton. We've all done everything by proxy, and the result is that I'm a regular fool about business. I think it's time I bought a little experience, and learned something about paddling my own canoe."

She smiled. "Experience in mining concessions is apt to be too expensive."

"But you'll keep me right," he said. "I can trust you."

"Not a bit of it," said Patricia. "I represent the seller. And you don't know me yet."

"I trust to my knowledge of faces," he said, but not priggishly. "Don't you?"

"No," said Patricia, promptly. "I've seen too many readily duplicated for that. If I understand you, you wish to buy into some concern which will occupy not only your money but your attention in Africa?"

"That's it."

"In this case the vendor wants ten thousand pounds down."

"I can run to that, if the thing is really good," he said.

"Very well. But afterwards you would require a survey. If that is satisfactory, there would be machinery to buy, a staff to pay, some years to wait for results, perhaps."

"We might get extra finance if all went well," he said. "I had your advertisement shown me last night by my cousin. He meant it as a joke, but I was rather taken by it."

"I think I had better see your solicitors all the same," said Patricia. "If you had been a business man, you would have had to take your chance, but this is like——"

"A slaughter of the innocents?" he suggested with a twinkle in his eye that rather surprised her. "But let me explain. My uncle, who died some months ago, was a funny old chap, very peppery, though one of the best. He had a quarrel with his solicitors before his death, and withdrew his business. His will was put in the hands of the Public Trustee."

"Then perhaps your money is tied?" she said.

"No, not at all. All the formalities are over. But this is the point: I haven't engaged other solicitors, have had no occasion to, so far. I asked my cousin Gage-Chipnell to act for me, but he refused. He's a solicitor, you know. He said relatives oughtn't to get into business relations."

"A wise man," said she. "But I can give you the names of several very sound lawyers."

She could see by the set of his chin that obstinacy was one of his little vices, and was not surprised when he replied:

"I was supposed to have been given a decent education, Miss Repton. It ought to enable me to understand any ordinary documents, oughtn't it?"

He spoke humorously, and she nodded. "Very well. On your

own head be it! I'll go through the documents with you now, and you must judge for yourself. By the way, did your uncle live at Chipnell Chase?"

"Yes. Do you know it?"

She shook her head, as she got up to fetch the papers. "No, but a cousin of an old friend of ours lives near there, and has spoken of it—Mr Elphinstone."

He started. "Jove! Of course. Richard Elphinstone of Craveley. My uncle knew him quite well."

Patricia turned from the safe with the bundle of documents in her hand. "Now, Mr Carey, this is business. We are on opposite sides, and you won't expect me to give a point away."

"The rigour of the game," smiled Carey.

She rang her bell for Miss Froud, and opened the bundle. As she passed him the first document, and spread out on the desk a map of the concession, Miss Froud came in.

"Write Mr Hanaper asking him to meet a client here tomorrow at eleven," Patricia instructed her. "You have the address."

Miss Froud went out. Patricia settled down to the business of the moment, and an hour and a half had passed before they were finished. Then she lit a cigarette, passed the box to Carey, and sat back.

"What do you think of it?"

Carey replied promptly and definitely, "OK, Miss Repton! I know we must rely on the expert's report at present, but he seems to have been rather a swell, doesn't he?"

"He was very well known."

"And, at the worst, this land has possibilities, even if the copper is missing?"

"I should think so. It is not swamp land, and a good many people are going out to Africa now."

"I'll buy it," said Carey, "I am quite keen on it. I am used to country life. I don't stay in town much. At present I am staying with my cousin at his flat in Cheyne Walk. I'd like you to meet him."

"You are beginning badly as a business man," said Patricia, "A

21

confession of keenness ought to be the last word on a buyer's lips!"

"You've taught me a lot already," he said, smiling at her admiringly.

"My commission on the deal will pay for the lessons," she said. "I draw it from the vendor, of course. But now I must say goodbye for the moment. Come tomorrow at eleven. I think it would be wise if you told Mr Gage-Chipnell what you have decided, though."

"Oh, I'll tell him," he said, as he got up and shook hands. "He's an awfully good sportsman, though so punctilious about business. He isn't much older than I am, you know."

When he had gone, Patricia sat smiling at her desk. It struck her that Peter Carey was exceedingly naïve, and at the same time very attractive. He was a man men could make a fool of, though she was not sure that women could.

At any rate, here was business at last. She glowed. Her first client had proved a winner. She hoped that, like a snowball, her affairs would gather weight and momentum as they rolled on.

CHAPTER 3 THE DEAL IS CLOSED

When Peter Carey turned up at the office next day he brought his cousin with him, though not, as he explained, in an official capacity.

Patricia found Mr Gage-Chipnell a pleasant man of twenty-nine, short but dapper, exceedingly well dressed, rather dark in colouring, with brown eyes, a small but determined mouth, the very model of a solicitor with a West-End practice. Mr Hanaper arrived almost simultaneously, a foil in his rough clothes to the two smartly attired men who awaited him.

He seemed well-pleased, and had shed some of his awkwardness which, Patricia guessed, had been the result of many rebuffs. They sat down at once to discuss matters. Hanaper explained some points in the documents that did not seem quite clear to the others; Gage-Chipnell looked about him, smiling.

"I have really no business to interfere at all," he said, in his light tenor voice, "but, since my cousin is disposed to consider the matter, I must say that the first payment of ten thousand pounds appears to me rather high. The engineer Gores was an excellent man, but Mr Carey has not seen the concession."

Hanaper bit his lip. "I want the money," he said diffidently. "But if Mr Carey won't buy unless——"

"Excuse me, Mr Hanaper," said Patricia sweetly, "I am representing you, and you must not compromise my position by making remarks of that kind."

Carey looked kindly at Hanaper. "Wait a moment," he said, "I haven't said what I think yet."

Mr Hanaper broke out again. "I'm sorry, miss, but I want to sell. I can't afford not to sell, if you know what I mean."

"I know perfectly well what you mean," said Patricia, thinking that he and Carey were two of a kind, "perfectly."

"A smaller sum, say," cooed Gage-Chipnell.

"Even a thousand would carry me along, if I could be sure of the other after," said Hanaper.

Patricia laughingly put her fingers in her ears. "It seems to me that Mr Gage-Chipnell and I are the only businesslike people here, though we happen to be on opposite sides."

"Look here," said Carey, "this proposition suits me. If the title is good, I am prepared to take it over. If I take it over, I am prepared to pay down what Mr Hanaper asks."

"I am ready to meet you half way, sir," said Hanaper eagerly. "I can trust you, sir, I see."

Peter Carey's obstinate chin stuck out a little. "Thank you, but I mean what I say—Hubert, I wish you would oblige me, and look through this stuff with a view to the legal side."

Gage-Chipnell sighed. "Well, old chap, if I must, I must; but without prejudice as regards taking any of your other legal business. Do you agree to that?"

"Of course," said Carey. "I suppose my cousin may have the documents to look over, Miss Repton?"

"He will sign a receipt for them," said Patricia. "Mr Hanaper naturally understands that you can't buy a pig in a poke."

"I quite understand, miss," said Hanaper gratefully.

Miss Froud was rung for, procured the copy of the list of documents, and returned with it. Gage-Chipnell took it and put it with the papers. "I think I may get along now," he added.

Hanaper got up. "Can I offer either of you gentlemen a drink?" he asked humbly. "Only too happy, you know, if——"

"Not for me, thank you," said the solicitor, smiling.

"And I want to talk a little matter over with Miss Repton," said

Carey.

Patricia smiled, shook hands with her client and the solicitor, and showed them out by the door leading direct into the corridor. Then she returned to Carey.

"Well; you have been generous," she said.

He shook his head awkwardly. "The poor chap looked so eager to get the cash," he said. "He looks as if he was worried."

She nodded. "Carrying this thing from pillar to post," she said. "A sickening job."

"But why should he?"

"Because the City is not so keen on potential mining propositions as you, Mr Carey. The average financier cannot pull up stakes and farm his concession if it does not prove metalliferous. Besides, the city is a bit full up with mining schemes just now, and won't touch them unless it can get them for a song."

"The kind of small song Hubert wanted me to sing just now," he said, with a touch of unexpected humour. "I know. But I'm not like that. Hubert was trained for his job, I wasn't. I was brought up at the Chase by my uncle. He hated business, and law. His idea of an education, when one was grown up, was to teach one to ride straight, hold a gun straighter, and sacrifice even pheasants for foxes. I think it a rotten system myself, if that is to be all, but the result of it is that I have imbibed some unbusinesslike notions."

Patricia smiled at him. He seemed to her so much a boy still, even in his anxiety to tell her something about himself.

"Your cousin was only doing what he should do," she said. "He thought you could get the thing at a cheaper cost. Now that you have made up your mind, I may tell you I think you could. You see, I have to take the strict view for my client too."

He nodded. "But I don't think you would let me in on a stumer."

She laughed. "Not if I knew it was one. Knowing that you are anxious to go out and farm, even if no more comes of it, I feel that you can't be let down. Mining propositions are always speculative."

"I know. I am not quite a fool, Miss Repton. If nothing comes of the copper, I pay no more than the ten thou, and I have a big whack of land for the money."

"That is so."

He nodded again. "Well, Mr Hanaper wants the money promptly. There will be no trouble about that. If Hubert advises me that the title is clear, I shall draw a cheque for the money at once, I want to get out as soon as I can."

Patricia rose. "Your cousin will let me know, no doubt. Now I must really get to work again."

He rose too, and looked at her awkwardly. "Will you lunch with me, Miss Repton?" he said diffidently.

She laughed. "It wouldn't do—look too like a conspiracy for the representative of the vendor and the buyer himself to lunch together! Thanks awfully, though. I should have loved to come in other circumstances."

He looked disappointed, but made no further attempt to persuade her. "I didn't know there was so much ceremony about business," he said. "But perhaps another time."

"We never know," said Patricia. "Goodbye, Mr Carey."

When Carey had gone, she sat for a few moments thinking happily. Her first deal had gone through. Her well-wishers had advised her against tackling this sort of job. They had tried to advise her for the best, but they had been mistaken. Her commission would come to a nice little sum.

Then again a doubt came to her. If this was all it should be, why had no one else taken it up! She smothered that doubt. After all, even the cleverest financiers did make mistakes. She rose, and rang up Mr Elphinstone.

"Pat Repton speaking," she said, when she recognised the old man's precise voice. "I just rang you up to shout 'Hurrah!'— Aren't you glad?"

"I hope to be, my dear, when I have heard what the hurrah portends," said he. "May I hear?"

"Money," said Patricia, gleefully. "I have just had a client, and a

26

visitor, and I have linked them up, and the result is that I draw commission on ten thousand pounds."

There was a moment's silence, then Mr Elphinstone replied, "I congratulate you, though I fear this success may make your acceptance of Jane's offer and mine further off than ever. But do come and tell us about it. This evening, eh? Come to dinner. Jane will be delighted."

"I'm sorry I can't tonight," said Patricia. "May I make it tomorrow night?"

"Do," said he. "But really your news astounds me. I never suspected that you would begin with business of this magnitude. Bravo, my dear! I hope it may only be the forerunner of many even greater successes."

"The old dear!" said Patricia, as she put down the receiver again. "I am really jolly lucky."

She went out to Miss Froud, who was sitting expectantly at her table.

"We win," she said, and the typist loved her for sharing the information. "If all goes well, the firm has clicked."

"Oh, I am so glad," said Miss Froud, "I began to wonder if I should really ever have any work to do."

"You will be complaining of too much soon," said Patricia. "At least, I hope so.—Have you ever been to the Savoy, Miss Froud?"

"Never," said the other.

"Ring up a taxi-cab and we'll go there now," said Patricia. "This is a thing to be celebrated with fatted calves and other delicacies. The firm must pat itself on the back occasionally!"

CHAPTER 4 HUBERT

Mrs Elphinstone was a plump, cheerful old lady, with shining white hair, and a staccato style of talking which was in strong contrast to her husband's rather formal speech.

When Patricia arrived at the house in Portland Place half an hour before dinner, she found her hostess already dressed, and sitting in the drawing-room waiting for her. Mr Elphinstone had not yet come down.

"My dear," said the old lady, kissing the girl warmly, "how clever you are! I knew it. I have always told James. How do you do this hey-presto work? You are amazing."

"Just a bit of luck," said Patricia, sitting down by her. "I was a lone female agent, and my client had been getting some rough stuff from the male financiers. He came to me, and——But I had better tell you all about it."

She gave Mrs Elphinstone a brief account of the transaction, and laughed. The old lady raised her eyebrows.

"It looks like magic, my dear. Very profitable magic. But so does something else—a coincidence. This Mr Gage-Chipnell is coming here, tonight to dine! Did anything more extraordinary ever happen?"

Patricia started. "Good gracious! But do you know him?"

Mrs Elphinstone smiled. "My dear, why not? But, as a matter fact, the acquaintance is only a day old. The young fellow called yesterday afternoon. It appears he knows my brother-in-law very well. James has heard his brother speak of him. Of course the Gage-Chipnells are well known in that part of the world. James invited him to dinner tonight."

Patricia bit her lip. "But how odd."

"Is it? I don't know. Or can he have fallen in love with you at first sight?"

"Our only meeting was brief and businesslike," said Patricia demurely.

"No doubt. But—did he know? Could he?"

"I told Mr Carey I knew you both."

The old lady threw up her hands. "That's it. Now I know why he was so suddenly anxious to make our acquaintance. Isn't it sad? I was hoping James and I were the cynosure of his eyes, and now it turns out to be you."

Patricia grinned. "What nonsense! I can see Mr Elphinstone has been giving you his views on marriage for businesslike spinsters."

As she spoke, Mr Elphinstone came in, and she had to go over the ground once more, to receive her old friend's congratulations again, and parry his laughing confirmation of his wife's views.

"Why not Mr Carey—if it is a question of marriage?" she asked.

"Speaking by the book," said Mrs Elphinstone, there are only two things that take men to Africa—big-game shooting, or a disappointment in love. From our fiction it seems to be a misogynists' paradise.—Your Mr Carey won't do."

Hubert Gage-Chipnell was announced then, and came in with his normal air of quiet assurance. He greeted his host and hostess, then bowed with some surprise to Patricia.

"Why, Miss Repton—you and I have met very lately," he said.

"You miss the pen behind my ear, perhaps?" said Patricia, flippantly, as she shook hands.

He smiled. "Don't you find it hard to keep up your end in the City?"

"I have only started, and I am not too badly pleased," said she.

Mr Elphinstone moved closer. "If we had only thought of it we might have asked you to bring your cousin," he said.

The lawyer smiled. "He is deep in preparations already. My flat is a litter of books on African travel, gun-makers' catalogues, and other things."

Mrs Elphinstone looked at him. "So you really think the thing is sound? Patricia has been telling us about it."

He bowed. "So far as I can see, it is all right, Mrs Elphinstone. He's very keen on going abroad. He's an impulsive fellow, you know."

"For my own sake and my client's, I am glad he is," said Patricia. "It's your money we want!"

During dinner Patricia had a better opportunity to study him. On the whole she liked him. He was well-informed, good-looking. He spoke affectionately of his cousin Peter Carey, but confessed that he did not know him very well.

"But I am sure of one thing," he said presently. "Going to a new country will make a man of him. He's a bit diffident, but he has it in him to be a man of action. A few years of roughing it will sharpen all his good qualities."

"He was brought up at the Chase, wasn't he?" asked the host.

"Yes, I struck out earlier, and I am afraid rather shocked my uncle. He had the old prejudice against lawyers; hardly trusted them. His own firm of lawyers found him a handful."

"But why did you take up the Law?" asked Patricia.

He laughed. "I always had a taste for it. Even at school I was in request as an arbitrator. The fellows used to call me 'The Attorney.' A pal of mine there went into the law—inherited a firm in fact—and I had a chance, you see."

"Do you ever regret it?" said Mr Elphinstone.

"On the whole, no. I have my share of the loaves and fishes. Besides, my tastes are purely urban. I am not a sportsman in the rural sense of the word."

"There are worse things," said Patricia.

"Much worse, but temperament, you know, has a say. Now you —I can see you better on a hunter than a revolving office chair."

"I am greedy," she laughed. "Also I have an idea that my office chair may bring me back to hunters."

"At the present rate we shall soon expect you to take over a mastership," said Mr Elphinstone, laughing. "But, talking of this business, I wonder why this concession has not been taken before? It seems a good thing gone begging."

"It may have been the appearance of the fellow," said Gage-Chipnell. "He looked wild and woolly."

"I thought all prospectors were," said Mrs Elphinstone. "I only see them on the screen, but isn't it so? Fur coats and snow-shoes. Knives and revolvers."

"That's Canada, barring the revolvers," said Patricia. "With the armoury, you must mean Alaska."

"I must, I suppose," said the hostess. "But is this young fellow going out alone? Does he know anything about it? My only knowledge of Africa is from a rhyme. A missionary and a cassowary, or something."

"Are you not thinking of the Lady from Riga and the tiger?" said Patricia gravely.

"My dear, no! Tigers are Indian. I know that. But with cassowaries about and other wild fowl, what will happen to your inexperienced traveller?"

Patricia looked across at her fellow-guest. He smiled. "Ah, that was a question in my own mind. I had far sooner he went out with a party—or someone who knew the ropes. I was wondering if it would not be wise to advertise in the *Field*. But I found an alternative."

"Not to go?" remarked Mrs Elphinstone.

"Oh no. He's going. Wild horses can't change Peter's mind once he has made it up. But it's this. I ran across a fellow today. I don't know him really. I met him, stayed in the same hotel with him once at Perth. A mighty hunter, don't you know, and at a loose end. He came in when I was lunching at Martin's today, and recognised me at once."

"What is he—professional bear-leader?" asked Patricia.

"By no means. I believe he has a bit of money, and a taste for the primitive. He's hanging about town on the chance of joining a party short of a man. I put it to him about Peter, provisionally of course, and he jumped at the idea."

"But does he know the part of Africa to which your cousin

proposes to go?" asked Mr Elphinstone.

"Fortunately he does. He says it is very much out of the way. He's a strange fellow. I imagine he has done a bit of elephant-poaching now and then. At any rate, he had to bolt once from the Belgians, and his line lay across that very country."

"It seems providential," remarked Mr Elphinstone.

The young man nodded and continued. "I thought so. He agrees that there is a chance of finding copper there, though he doesn't pretend to be a mine man. But he can help Peter order what is needed on this side, and take charge of the expedition on the other. That means a lot, I believe. A fellow taking over a lot of natives will get stung; even if he doesn't get left, Townard says. They draw some cash in advance, and fade away in the bush the first day or two."

"Have you told your cousin?" asked Patricia.

"I haven't seen him today. He went away to a gun-fitter to get fitted for some rifles. He's as keen as mustard."

"I suppose he will have to pay for the privilege?" said the hostess. "I mean this man Townard."

"Yes, but dirt cheap. The fellow's hankering to get back to the wilds, and he'll go for ten a month—and his keep, of course."

The subject dropped. Mrs Elphinstone retired with Patricia to the drawing-room.

"Now, my dear," she said when they sat down, "I am sure I was right. The young man is *rusé*. He couldn't keep his eyes off your face. I saw that. He looked us up the moment he knew we knew of his people. What do you think of him?"

"Competent," said Patricia smiling.

"That won't do at all. No one marries a man for his competence. Competence is not fascinating."

"What about the lure of the strong silent man?"

"It may be, but Mr Gage-Chipnell is not silent. You heard him talk of the loaves and fishes. Now, while competence is not essential in matrimony, loaves and fishes are."

"I've just baked a little loaf of my own."

"I know. But don't get too proud about it. A niece of mine once

32

made an excellent cake. It was her only one."

"A friend of mine married the wrong man," said Patricia. "She is sorry she has one. No; I must try out my baking before I give up."

"I think he is nice," said Mrs Elphinstone.

"And shows good taste," added Patricia.

Mr Elphinstone and his guest came in presently, and the talk turned on mutual friends. It turned out that the lawyer knew several of the Elphinstones' friends in town.

"I must have heard of you," said the hostess presently. "Are you the gifted person who sings like a lark?"

"For a lark, perhaps. I have never flown high."

"James," said Mrs Elphinstone, "you remember that tiresome man who insisted that Mr Gage-Chipnell was as good as a professional? I insist on a test! Patricia, I know you accompany."

Patricia grinned. "I can vamp."

The lawyer smiled. "If you insist, Mrs Elphinstone. Or ought I to say that I have a cold, and wait to be persuaded?"

Patricia walked over to the piano and sat down, "I have suffered too often from persuading people," she said. "What shall it be?"

She saw that this was a point of vanity with the man. Whether he sang ill or well, he was proud of his voice. She found his general air of assurance not unpleasant. It was not so much impudence as competence. Mrs Elphinstone had found the right word. Peter Carey's diffidence would have sat ill on him, and there she found a clue to the difference between the cousins. Peter had given an invitation, and been put off with a refusal; Hubert had found his way here to see her, unless her hostess was much mistaken.

"I have no music with me," said he, as he joined her. Patricia went through a number of songs, and presently he picked out a song by Reynaldo Hahn.

"I think I know this," he said, and stuck it up on the piano rest.

He had a charming light tenor voice, and sang with taste and finish.

"How clearly one hears your words," said Mrs Elphinstone, when the song had come to an end. "But I admit I don't care for that kind of song. My husband loves it. I am dramatic by nature. I want to be stirred up, not to feel artistic."

"Verdi?" said he, smiling at her.

"How did you know? You are a magician. Music with knives in it, or sobs, or both."

"Then Leoncavallo is even better for you," he replied. "I wonder if you have 'Vesti la giubba'?"

Mrs Elphinstone chuckled. "You are a dangerous man! A thought-reader, perhaps. That is exactly what I should like."

Patricia delved deeper into the pile of music and brought this up. "Now for the sob in the voice," she said. "Mrs Elphinstone will never forgive you if you leave that out." She sat on the stool and looked at the old lady. "Do you remember Dick Caley singing it? He made 'On with the motley' sound like 'Yes, we have no bananas'!"

"Or as if he was a man who has at last found a chance to divorce his wife, but has to pretend to be frightfully cut up about it."

"Your demands are exacting," laughed the singer, "but I can only do my best."

His best entranced Mrs Elphinstone. He sang with great feeling, slightly dramatising the song, but that was not out of place here. Patricia listened with amazement. The self-assured and composed man seemed to show a heart here. If he was vain about his voice he had some grounds for it.

"You sing delightfully," she said when he had finished.

"Thank you," he said, his eyes on her, his face slightly flushed. "Your accompaniment was such a help. I knew I could rely on you."

"Your tiresome friend was right," said the hostess to her husband. "Mr Gage-Chipnell, you must come and sing to our friends one evening. Make it soon!"

"Delighted," he said as he sat down. "But, by the way, I have a little plan that will give me much pleasure if you can fall in

34

with it. It's merely a theatre, for which I have the promise of a box. Would you and Mr Elphinstone—perhaps Miss Repton too—come with me?"

"Delighted," said Mr Elphinstone. "That is, of course, if we are not engaged."

"Friday," he said.

"No, that is not one of our engaged evenings," said his hostess. "We will go if you will dine here first. What about you, Pat?"

Patricia nodded. "Thank you. I'd love to."

He had said nothing about Peter Carey, and she wondered.

"By the way, have you really advised Mr Carey to buy?" she asked a little later, when she rose to go.

"I have," he said. "Oh, Miss Repton, my car is coming round in a few minutes. Can I drop you anywhere?"

"Thank you. I am going straight home."

He nodded. "It is on my way, I think," he said.

As Patricia put on her things upstairs, she wondered how he knew. Her office address, of course, but she had not told him where she lived. He must have looked it up, just as he had hastened to look up her friends. She was flattered. Even a young woman gifted with considerable common sense may be flattered without being ashamed of it when she produces such an instant impression.

"I don't think he would have accepted my refusal to lunch so easily," she thought with a smile, as she went downstairs to the car.

When she stepped in, she was reminded again of Mrs Elphinstone's reference to the loaves and fishes. It was an expensive and handsome car, and a neatly uniformed chauffeur was in the driving seat. For a young lawyer he must be doing more than well.

CHAPTER 5 THE DEAL IS COMPLETED

"Well, gentlemen," said Patricia on the Friday morning, "I think that completes the business. Mr Hanaper, you will perhaps leave me an address at which I can always find you. It may be a considerable time before anything definite can be done in the matter of exploiting any minerals."

Mr Hanaper looked at her gratefully. "I must thank you, miss, for the way you have helped me and done this business for me," he said. "I was wondering if this gentleman here would mind looking after my interests for me? I never know when I may not be going away."

Slightly surprised by this request, Gage-Chipnell looked hard at the prospector. "I? Oh, I don't know." He looked round at Peter Carey, and added to him, "Of course, Peter, I told you I was only going to look over this thing for you."

"I know," said Peter. "I have no objection to your acting for Mr Hanaper now. It's all settled, so there is no snag."

Mr Hanaper beamed. "Then, if I may, sir, I'll come on to your office later."

He had received his cheque and given a receipt for it. He shook hands all round now, in a grateful but awkward fashion, put on his hat, took it off again, and left.

"A rough diamond," said Peter, as the door closed. "Well, I am an African proprietor now, I think, Miss Repton. I am awfully bucked about it too. Did you hear that I have come across a fellow who knows all the ropes out there?"

"Mr Gage-Chipnell told me," said Patricia.

"This morning?" said Peter.

His cousin smiled. "How ridiculous of me! I forgot to tell you, old chap. I looked up the Elphinstones the other day, and, by the oddest coincidence, met Miss Repton there. Which reminds me, they are going to the theatre tonight with me. Will you come?"

Peter shook his head. "Why, old chap, you fixed up that appointment with Townard for this evening—at least I thought you did."

"I had forgotten that, too. Perhaps you could put him off?"

Carey shook his head. "I shouldn't like to. He seems so keen on the job. But, look here, won't you both lunch with me today? I asked Miss Repton before, but it seemed there were lions in the path, or something."

"Of course I'll be glad," said his cousin. "Do let us celebrate your first stroke of business, Miss Repton."

Patricia laughed and agreed. Peter beamed on her, and they went down to the car that had brought him and his cousin to the office. On their way to the hotel where they were to lunch, Peter told her eagerly all about his plans, his rifles, his outfit. He was like a boy in his anxiety to get her opinion. Beside him Gage-Chipnell seemed the complete man of the world. But there was something fascinating too about Peter's ingenuousness, his impulsiveness and friendliness. They were not those of a fool, but merely an expression of his temperament.

"He's like a boy with a new hoop, isn't he?" said his cousin indulgently. "Peter, you are horribly like your name."

Peter grinned. "That isn't my fault, old boy. But here we are."

The older man left him to do most of the talking as they lunched. He studied Patricia quietly, while his cousin excitedly discussed his plans. But that might have been because he knew he would have Patricia near him at dinner, and beside him in the box that night. If he made a mistake, it was in thinking that boyishness is boring rather than refreshing.

He knew that he had a fine voice, and he was well aware that

Peter would have showed badly against him in sophisticated society. He knew the advantages he had, not least his faculty for knowing when to take the bull by the horns, and when not to accept an unmeant refusal.

For Mrs Elphinstone had been right. He had timed that visit to her with a purpose in view. Knowing a good many women, he had been caught at once by one who differed from them in so many ways. He had laughed at himself for falling so easily, but the laugh did not change his opinion. He found something provocative about her. He could not say what it was, but it spurred him on. He meant to make the running, and ignored Peter as a factor altogether.

"I know Hubert will think me potty," Peter was saying, "but I closed down with old Townard at once. He is a jolly interesting fellow. I never heard such yarns, but I, somehow, imagine most of 'em are true."

"Wild tales of Araby," said Patricia.

"And beyond," said Peter.

"There!" Hubert was laughing at his cousin. "He sees the man once, and actually fixes up an arrangement with him. But I thought you said you were making an evening appointment with him, Peter."

"So I am. He says there is always the dickens of a lot to do in these expeditions—worse than in China almost. He says you get your men and then you can't get your stores. When you get your stores, you find some of the men have gone. When you get fresh men, it's next year! So he proposes that I should bundle him off well in advance, and when I arrive he'll have some of the donkey-work done."

Patricia looked at him. "Not a bad idea, but I hope you are not taking on this man too hastily."

Peter shook his head. "I told you I went by faces. He's a sound sportsman, and anxious to save my money, too. He insists on going out by a cheaper steamer. He has a bit of his own, you know."

"When does it sail?" asked Hubert.

"Next Wednesday. Don't laugh! If I fix up, there is no use in wasting time, is there?"

"It has just occurred to me that you might have engaged Hanaper," said Hubert. "He actually found the place, so he could be even more valuable."

Peter shrugged. "Too late. I can't dangle this before Townard's nose, then leave him in the air. Besides, I like him." He turned to Patricia with his diffident smile. "I am awfully sorry I can't come to the theatre. I should have liked to have seen something more of you."

Hubert roared. "There's directness for you!" he cried. "Miss Repton, didn't I tell you Peter was a man of action?"

Patricia smiled at Carey. She liked his way of putting it, and was flattered by it more than she would have cared to show his sophisticated cousin.

"I am sorry too," she said.

Peter nodded. "I must learn the art of polishing my sentiments and phrases," he said. "Hubert, I think, has a stock ready for use."

"That's unkind," said his cousin. "A nasty one for me. But I'm sure we're both sorry you can't join us."

Patricia felt sure that Peter would stay after Hubert had gone. To her surprise he said goodbye when his cousin did, and, though she thought she caught a disappointed look on his face, he did not suggest accompanying her back to the office. Perhaps he might have done so had not Hubert put the car at her disposal, and told the driver to take her back to the city.

"He's nice," said Pat to herself, as she sat down in her office chair once more. "But they're both nice fellows. I think his cousin is the sounder, but Peter is more attractive."

More unusual was what she meant. Most of the young men she knew were on the same model as Gage-Chipnell, while Carey had a tinge of the latter-day backwoodsman in him.

She dined as promised, with the Elphinstones, found Hubert there, and was again struck by his solicitude for Peter Carey. He was anxious that the expedition should be a success, but inclined apparently to feel that more haste might mean less speed.

"As I told you, he is a boy still," he said to her. "But I suppose he will be all right. Cotton-wool is a bad wrapping in the African climate."

"I don't think he needs it," said Patricia. "He may be boyish, but there is a look in his eyes that shows he won't be fooled long."

"What business have you to be looking into his eyes, Pat?" asked Mrs Elphinstone gaily. "Perhaps you can tell us what colour they are?"

"My dear!" murmured her husband, who was always inclined to frown on levity.

Patricia laughed. "I won't tell you! One must have some secrets. Meanwhile, I am not so much thinking of the colour of Mr Carey's eyes as the play we are going to see. Is it funny or serious?"

Hubert nodded. "Some people say it is funny. Go prepared to weep, and you may find it screaming."

"The best way with funny plays," said Mrs Elphinstone. "If you go with a laugh between your lips, it never seems to get any further."

"Which reminds me, my dear," said her husband, with fussy irrelevance, "that it is time you got ready."

Patricia was one of the people who did not find that play funny. It was like a bad cracker: nice to look at, plenty of pull on both sides, but no crack for a culmination. But she sat next to Hubert, and he kept her amused during the many longueurs, and proved an even more excellent companion than she had hoped.

That he was impressed by her was evident. He showed that in many ways, though he did not even venture on the rim of a flirtation. He did not tell her about himself, as Peter had done; though that might not be the result of a lack of vanity, but of tactics born of experience.

When they dropped Patricia at home, she thanked him for the evening very warmly, and did not refuse when he suggested that she might come for a run with him in his car one day.

"I should like it," she said, as she shook hands.

"I am sorry the play was a wash-out," he said. "Not quite a wash-out for me, though—rather the reverse."

She smiled mischievously. "Then you must go to see it again," she remarked. "Goodnight."

Mrs Elphinstone was a most remarkable matchmaker. It was not that she made many matches, but those that she aspired to make absorbed all her attention, and led her to extravagant attempts to bring them off. Her first duty, on putting Patricia on the roster of those-who-ought-to-be-married, was to look up Peter Carey in a book of reference devoted to country gentlemen, then to telephone to her brother-in-law at Cravely for further information.

Peter, it seemed, was the heir when his uncle died, and was now in possession of Chipnell Chase.

"Which is odd, since the other cousin's name is Chipnell," she told her husband.

"We have heard of favourite sisters and unliked brothers," her husband commented. "You may be sure that is the case here. A Carey married old Gage-Chipnell's sister. We hear the boy was brought up at the Chase."

"Quite," said Mrs Elphinstone. "The estate must be worth two hundred thousand pounds at least, from what your brother tells me."

"I don't quite see the point of this," said he mildly.

"I suppose not, my dear. But I see it. Mr Gage-Chipnell is a promising lawyer. Mr Carey is a landowner and a wealthy man. He would be much more suitable for Pat."

Her husband stared. "Bless my soul, my dear! The young fellow is going to Africa."

"But not for ever," she said calmly. "I must have him here. I want to have a look at him. You must write."

"But I don't know him, Jane."

"You will when he comes. Ask him to tea on Sunday. I will telephone to Pat and ask her to come."

"But will that not be unusual, unconventional?"

"Both, perhaps. But I despair of you, James. You tell me you think Patricia ought to get married. I am doing my best for her. I can see she thinks Mr Carey charming. Very well. Write to Mr Carey!"

It was done. On that morning, Mr Elphinstone wrote to Mr Carey, squirming in his precise way as he did it. Mrs Elphinstone telephoned to Patricia's office immediately after breakfast to ask her to come to tea next day.

Miss Froud answered the phone. She said that her employer had not yet reached the office, but would tell her when she came in.

"At four," said the old lady.

"I will remember," said Miss Froud, and went back to her typing table wondering if she should not have said "shall" instead of "will." They laid great stress on these points at the school where she had been educated.

But, if Mr Elphinstone's invitation was unconventional when directed to a stranger, the stranger received it with fervent gratitude.

"Perhaps Miss Repton didn't think me quite such an ass as Hubert does," he said to himself, as he read the note. "Hang it all! I wish I hadn't met her just when I had made up my mind to go abroad!"

He really was not less keen on his African visit, but it was just as he had said. Even unsophisticated men do not think it possible in real life to snatch a bride in a few days and take her to share their adventures. Still, he had never been able to get Patricia out of his mind since the morning when he had entered the office and found the financial agent a young woman of charm.

Just how highly he had appraised that charm he did not tell Hubert. Something stopped him there. Impulsive and frank as he was, he felt that he would be laughed at.

On the Sunday he went to the Elphinstones' in a mood of exultation. He liked Mrs Elphinstone and her husband, and they liked him. But Patricia did not turn up. She had not turned up on the Saturday morning at her office, so Miss Froud's message had remained undelivered.

"I never knew her fail me before," said Mrs Elphinstone, when it was a quarter past four. "I'll ring her up at home."

She came back with a blank face. Patricia had left in a car, with a gentleman, at two o'clock.

"Your cousin, I suppose," she said to Peter.

Peter's face fell. "I shouldn't be surprised," said he.

CHAPTER 6 STRATEGY

Patricia herself was never certain if Peter Carey avoided her, or chance arranged that he and she should be always in different places, or held by engagements when they might have met.

Hubert Gage-Chipnell might have told her. He knew where his cousin was going and when, and she did not. He was assiduous as a cavalier, acted on the motto that all was fair in love and war, and generally managed to be with Patricia when Peter had leisure and the inclination to emulate him.

Mrs Elphinstone suspected this, and did her best to make a diversion. But she had nothing against Hubert, and was not assisted with sufficient energy by her favourite, who was inclined to wait for encouragement instead of making it, not because he was complacent, but because he was lacking in the assurance that might have carried him forward. Also he had the man Townard to see, details to arrange, and this could not be done in a minute.

After all, Townard did not go on the cheaper boat, but had to postpone his sailing to the following Friday. Peter was tied a good deal by this necessary satellite.

Patricia was not sure where she stood. Indeed, she had not yet had time to get her bearings. It's nonsense to assume that people know the moment they fall in love, or if they have fallen in love at all. Infatuations and passions that lead nowhere, emotional sky-rockets are unmistakable. But love has no burned-out stick, and equally is not set up carefully and touched off with a match. It is bad enough not to know when you are in love, but far worse not to know when you are not.

Hubert had some attractive ways. He was charming, he knew how to look after the modern young woman, when not to fuss, when to go away, when to arrive. He had a way of making any woman feel that she was the woman but not the only woman in the world.

To be told you are the only woman is to derive things of the competitive charm. The only woman in the world is bound to fascinate all the men in it. Hubert appeared to be telling her that feminine charm was abundant not rare. He flattered her by his preference.

She did not suspect that he had almost succeeded in eliminating Peter from her scheme of things. Peter began to fade. You do not quicken or improve an acquaintance by absence.

"You are never here when he comes," said Mrs Elphinstone.

"Or is it that he is never here when I come?" said Patricia.

"Don't quibble!" said the old lady. "I like him better than your lawyer."

"I don't know if I do," said Patricia.

"Then, my dear, you stay tonight. I have asked him to dinner. I really insist. Poor Mr Carey shall not go empty away every time he comes."

Patricia laughed. "Can I go home to change, or are you afraid I shall run away and not come back?"

The old lady's eyes twinkled. "If you give your parole, you may go, my dear. But don't let me hear that Mr Gage-Chipnell intercepted you on the way and took you off."

"I'll try to avoid him," said Pat. "What a desperate lady-killer you must think him!"

As she went home she was telling herself that she would like to meet Peter again. It was just accident that had prevented her from seeing him on the occasions when he had called at the Elphinstones'. He was going away too soon. She was sorry. She remembered his remark that he would like to see more of her. Hubert had laughed at that, but it was sincerely meant.

She returned later to the house in Portland Place, wearing her smartest frock in honour of Peter. But Peter did not turn up until it was nearly dinner time, and then, to her mingled surprise and amusement, Hubert was with him. It appeared that Mr Elphinstone had met the latter that day and asked him to come.

But Patricia was still more surprised to see that the two cousins looked grave and serious. Even Mrs Elphinstone noticed it and rallied them.

"Has the vibration at last shaken down St Paul's?" she asked.

Peter forced a smile. "We didn't notice it," he said.

Mr Elphinstone had come home late from his club, and hurried upstairs to dress without speaking to his wife. He entered now, as dinner was announced, and shook hands with Peter and Hubert. He, too, looked more grave than usual, and Patricia began to wonder if the two men had approached her old friend with regard to her.

"That must be my vanity," she mused, as Mr Elphinstone gave her his arm. "I don't suppose either of them thought of such a thing."

But the host had hardly seated himself at the head of the table before be made a remark which explained his mood.

"Have you heard of this extraordinary occurrence?" he asked, looking first at Peter and then at Patricia. "It came through on the tape just before I left my club."

"Do you mean about Mr Hanaper?" asked Hubert hurriedly.

"Mr Hanaper? Why, what has he done?" cried Patricia.

Peter turned to her. "He's dead! It's in the late edition. It's a terrible affair altogether."

"Who is Mr Hanaper?" demanded Mrs Elphinstone.

No one replied to her directly. Hubert was looking across the table at Patricia, his eyes thoughtful.

"It looks like murder," he said, in his even voice. "What do you think, Mr Elphinstone?"

Mr Elphinstone shook his head. "I should say suicide."

"But why should he commit suicide when he had that money?" asked Peter.

Patricia bit her lip and shivered a little. "Murder or suicide?"

46

Mrs Elphinstone motioned the servant to take away her untouched soup plate. "Isn't that like your sex?" she said. "All of you! I want to know who Mr Hanaper is. No one tells me. I want to know what happened. You all begin discussing probabilities. What about facts for a change."

Hubert nodded. "We haven't many, Mrs Elphinstone. There is a bare account in the newspaper this evening. But Mr Hanaper was Miss Repton's client. Peter paid him ten thousand pounds the other day. Now he has been found in his bed-sitting room at Willesden, shot through the head."

"How disgusting!" said Mrs Elphinstone.

"Poor man," murmured Patricia. "He had had such a hard time, and now, just when he succeeds, he comes to this."

"Extremely sad," said Mr Elphinstone.

"Still I am in the dark," said Peter. "If the poor chap had blown his brains out as the result of trying in vain to peddle his concession all round the City, I could understand it. But that ten thousand meant comfort. It beats me."

Hubert shook his head. "He went through hardships, I suppose. They may have shaken him. The reaction, you know ——"

"That's it," said Mrs Elphinstone. "Sudden joy following on depression. I can see that."

Patricia pulled herself together. The death of the man she had dealt with such a short time before had made a deep impression on her, but she was composed again when she spoke.

"Aren't we rather going too fast? Mr Carey, you have seen the evening paper, I suppose. Were there no other details?"

"Very few, Miss Repton. But Mr Elphinstone is right. It does look like suicide, for the revolver was found in the room with one chamber fired, and apparently his landlady knew he had a revolver."

"I suppose one needs them in Africa?" asked the hostess.

"One may," said Hubert. "But really that ends the evidence so far. The police have taken it up, of course, and we shall hear more tomorrow."

Patricia looked at Peter. "How do you stand? I don't see that it affects your position. The money was paid over and the documents signed."

Peter shrugged. "What do you say, Hubert?"

"That you are quite all right, old chap. But here is a point for some of us. I shouldn't worry about it, only that it involves Miss Repton."

"What do you mean?" asked the old lady excitedly.

"Nothing very serious. But here it is: ought any one of us to come forward and offer evidence? Miss Repton may not like that, or the publicity attached to a case of this kind. She is not obliged to come forward, as I see it."

Patricia frowned. "I don't know. It depends what the verdict is."

Hubert nodded. "Quite. I mean that you might at least wait until the inquest has taken place. If he committed suicide, I don't think our business with him can throw any light on the matter."

"But if, by any chance it should prove to be murder, there is still a great objection to Patricia giving evidence," said Mr Elphinstone in a shocked voice. "Nowadays there are the pressmen, the photographers; all the disgusting columns about the affair. I should hate that for her."

Patricia shook her head. "I believe every good citizen ought to help the law," she said. "If anything I can say will throw a ray of light on the affair, I shall certainly say it. I don't want that kind of advertisement, but I won't back out for that reason."

"Bravo!" said Peter.

"I quite agree with Miss Repton," said Hubert, "but we must wait. I repeat that. If the coroner's jury find suicide, the affair will wind itself up without our help."

"You forget Miss Repton's letter, or letters, to him," said Peter.

"So I did," said Hubert. "The police may find those."

Mr Elphinstone shook his head. "Perhaps the account that came over the tape was more full and precise than that vouchsafed to the evening press. I understood that the grate was full of burned papers."

48

"Then it was suicide," said Mrs Elphinstone.

Patricia nodded. "That does look like it. My letter may have been burned too. I shall certainly volunteer nothing until I hear what is said at the inquiry."

"I suppose he did not mention any enemies to you?" said Hubert.

"No. Well, he gave me the impression that he was not exactly liked by the Belgians, or Portuguese, in Africa, but that is a thing one can understand. I expect these foreign officials are inclined to suspect British prospectors of trying to cut into their profits, or snatch concessions from under their noses."

"So Townard told me," said Peter readily. "It's a game of catch-as-catch-can out there, and the nations rather scowl at one another across their borders, though their home governments may be friendly enough."

Patricia suddenly remembered M de Villegaile, and that tell-tale, half-erased comment she had found on the margin of one of Hanaper's documents. But she did not dwell on it, for all the evidence pointed to suicide so far, and it would not do to make a mountain out of a molehill.

Mr Elphinstone chimed in, "Do you good people mind if we drop the subject for the present? I do not see that any good purpose can be served by discussing it."

Mrs Elphinstone smiled at him. "James, you are inhuman! We are fallible mortals who like a mystery. We are all sorry for the poor man. That goes without saying. But I find it interesting."

Patricia patted the old lady's arm. "I'll come and tell you all about it every day. I hope it isn't murder, for that seems even more hateful than suicide, but, if it is, I'll do my best to help catch the criminal."

"On that side I will support you," said her host. "There is today far too much sympathy with the criminal, and not enough for the wronged. Petitions for the reprieve of murderers are common, and no one seems to think twice of the dead man's relatives."

The subject presently dropped, but the event had cast a gloom over the little dinner-party, and when they had retired to the drawing-room it hung undispelled in the atmosphere. Hubert did his best to be bright. Mrs Elphinstone tried to enliven them, but the three guests rose to go half an hour before the usual time for departing, and their host and hostess did not try to detain them. Only Mrs Elphinstone spoke ruefully to Patricia when they were upstairs together.

"There, my dear! There seems to be some fatality about it. I get Mr Carey here, and someone commits suicide and spoils things! But we must try again. What about next week?"

"Let me know in good time," said Patricia. "I do my best, you know."

It was again Hubert's car that took her away. But Peter was with them too, this time. If he was disappointed because he had seen so little of Patricia, he did not show it. Perhaps Hubert's former smile at his naïveté had put him off; perhaps the death of Mr Hanaper worried him.

"Does Mr Townard go soon?" Patricia asked him.

"At once," he said. "If Hubert says I am all right, there is no need to delay. If there had been any question of my title not being all right, it would have been a different matter."

"As I told you, it doesn't affect you, Peter."

"Good. But I am sorry for that poor devil. Years of struggling to get hold of that thing, then sale, and now snuffed out. He looked sound enough to me."

"Malaria, perhaps," said Patricia. "I believe it is depressing when it recurs."

"Very likely," said Peter. "I'll not forget my own quinine when I go out."

"I had almost forgotten that you were actually going out," Patricia remarked, as the car stopped at her place.

Peter looked at her. "I'm very keen on it," he said.

But Patricia almost thought that his tone was doubtful, or if not doubtful, at least unenthusiastic.

CHAPTER 7 THE BELGIAN EXPLAINS

Patricia read the fuller accounts of the tragedy in the morning paper next day, and made up her mind to visit Mr E de Villegaile. Nothing in the detailed accounts appeared to disprove the suicide theory, but the fact that E de V had annotated the dead man's document made her uneasy.

At ten o'clock she was at the offices of the Belgian company, and five minutes later she was talking to a dapper little Belgian, who was a model of politeness, and much more frank than she had expected him to be.

"You remember I rang you up asking you if you would care to look into an African mining proposition near Bangele?" she said presently. "Well, I sold it."

"I congratulate madame—or is it mademoiselle?" he smiled.

"So far only mademoiselle," she said with a twinkle. "But now I come to a strange thing. When I was examining the document in connection with that business, I came across a half-erased pencil note in the margin—initialled."

He bowed. "Not uncommon, mademoiselle."

"Far from it, I am sure. But those initials were 'E de V.'"

He smiled, undisturbed. "I share them with not a few of my compatriots, not to speak of Frenchmen. But you interest me. May I request the name of the vendor?"

"Hanaper," she said. "I understood that you had never been offered this proposition."

"You—you thought that might be—shall we say inexact, mademoiselle. I cannot regard that as a compliment."

"And you must not regard it as an insult," she said. "Please."

He stared hard at her. "Is this the unfortunate man who is dead? I see it in my paper this morning?"

"It is. Now, monsieur, the odd thing is this. You very kindly wrote an answer to my inquiry. The initial letters of your name corresponded to those on the margin of the document—I mean the handwriting itself."

If she expected him to start, she was mistaken. "A moment, mademoiselle," he said, and rang a bell. "I may have a letter filed that throws some light on that."

A clerk came in, and was given an instruction. De Villegaile turned again to his visitor.

"I remember I had a letter from that man asking me would I consider the affair. I wrote to say yes. I saw no more of him. May I ask what this marginal note said?"

"It was to the effect that Mr Hanaper was wrong, that this concession was in Belgian territory."

He did start this time. "Absurd. Zut! Why, mademoiselle, I told you myself there was no question about it being on our side."

The clerk returned with a letter, and retired again. The Belgian passed it to Patricia. "You see, mademoiselle? This man had an opportunity to study my writing."

She nodded. "But why should he forge a note by you on the margin of a document, and why should that note comment adversely on the concession?"

He smiled. "You are new to the City—no? I have an idea. It is that our friend, now dead, was certain that you would say to him that this was a good thing. You would wonder why he had not taken it elsewhere."

"He said he had," said Patricia, beginning to see light.

"*Sans doute*. Among others, he says he has showed it to me, and there I am saying so on the margin! But if I erase a note, I erase it. I am known here as one who has to do with African mining; he says I saw it, therefore he forges a note, which makes you assume that I reject this affair because it is situated on territory to which he can have no title. He knows that you will query this, and receive the right reply. He does not know that you will come to see me. No, he tells himself that you are a woman, women are fools, so you are a fool—a syllogism, mademoiselle, as foolish as most."

"But I am a fool!" cried Patricia. I was taken in. I sold the concession to someone."

"It does not follow that this is bad. But a rogue who plays such tricks may have tried to cheat you. I am sorry it is so. Only, if your client has paid the money, then I should not assume at once that it is wrong."

Patricia assented. "Ten thousand pounds changed hands over it."

He smiled. "Then I shall not be surprised if this man was killed for the money. Rogues are often watched by other rogues. If he had this money, also an accomplice, one sees the temptation."

Patricia talked with him for a minute or two more, then thanked him warmly for his help and went back to her office. Mr E de V had gone from the case as an important factor. Hanaper had tried a subtle trick, and carried it off with his diffident airs, and his rough, unsophisticated appearance. And now he was dead, and the Belgian's idea that he might have been murdered for his ill-gotten gains seemed not unlikely.

She was ill at ease as she entered her office. She had been so proud of her first coup, actually boasted of it to the Elphinstones, and now it seemed that she had been tricked by a confidence man of sorts. The fellow who would forge a marginal note might be expert enough to forge all the documents on which she had relied. Had she let Peter Carey down, sold him a pup by proxy? The thought was very bitter.

She took up a paper, and noticed that the inquest was to be held that day. In the ordinary course of things an inquiry of that kind was the last thing she would have cared to visit, but in the new circumstances she determined to go. It seemed to her that a woman starting in business as a financial agent must be at once marked down by rogues as easy money. Her mind registered an aphorism minted for the occasion: "Never trust a man because he looks awkward and wears badly-made clothes!"

She arrived at the place where the inquest was to be held and found it crowded. The jury had been sworn, the landlady at the Willesden lodgings had given most of her evidence, and was adding with hesitation the fact that she believed Mr Hanaper had kept a pistol. But then she thought folk from wild parts never went without one.

"What do you mean by *thinking* he kept one?" asked the Coroner. "Don't you know?"

"I saw one in a drawer once," said the good woman.

"Well, why didn't you say so? Now take a look at the weapon found in the dead man's room. Does it correspond to the one you saw?"

The landlady handled the weapon in a way that showed she hardly knew one end from the other.

"It looks the same size, sir," she said.

An officer got up in court. It appeared that the police had worked quickly and had luck as well. A gunsmith was in attendance to give evidence. The Coroner nodded, and the doctor who had been called in to see the dead man went into the stand.

His evidence was brief and businesslike. He had found Mr Hanaper, as he understood the dead man to be called, lying in the middle of the floor in a room in the Willesden house. He had been dead twenty minutes or so. The cause of death was a gunshot wound. The bullet had entered the middle of the forehead and penetrated the brain.

"In ordinary circumstances, you would have assumed that this wound was self-inflicted?" said the Coroner.

"Undoubtedly," answered the doctor. "I am still under that impression."

He gave grounds for the assumption. The bullet had entered the forehead just between, but slightly above the line of the eyebrows and travelled upwards.

"But I understand that there were no signs of burning, or blackening?" was the next question.

"No. That is the only difficulty. But, while I could not say definitely that the wound was the effect of a voluntary effort to destroy himself on the part of this man, I see no reason to doubt that it was due to his handling a loaded revolver."

"You refer to an accidental discharge?"

"Yes. The weapon was not found beside the dead man, but two yards away. My theory is that it dropped from his hand, and exploded, the bullet striking him in the face as he bent over. The recoil might have made the weapon jump on the floor."

"We shall have the gunsmith's evidence on that point," said the Coroner, and dismissed the witness after a few trifling questions.

A police officer next gave evidence about being called to the house and seeing the body. He was followed by a Detective-Inspector, who swore that he had searched the room, had found in a suitcase a bundle of Bank of England notes to the value of nine thousand six hundred and fifty-five pounds. He had discovered piles of ashes in the grate, practically all burned papers, and all completely incinerated.

The room was on the first floor of the house, at the back in what is known as a "return." The window was open, but it had been a warm night, and his investigations led him to believe that no one had entered the room by that means. There was no down-pipe near the window, there were no signs on the window-ledge, sill, or sashes to suggest an intruder. The return consisted of two storeys only, ground and first floor, though the house proper had three.

"Could not someone have descended by means of a rope?" the Coroner inquired.

The Inspector shook his head. "The rain-gutter above is very rotten and shaky, sir. If the notes had been missing, it would have been another story. A person who was washing up in the kitchen immediately below the bedroom will give evidence that she did not hear any sound of struggle above, but only the footsteps of one man, and then a crash and a thud."

This further evidence was then given, and after that a bearded little man gave evidence about the weapon found in the room. He swore that he had seen the body and identified it as that of a man who had visited his shop to get a revolver repaired. From his talk he believed him a South African who was going out again immediately. He had undertaken to clean the action and oil it for this customer. He had done so, and the man had called for it a week before his death. He identified that weapon as the one now in court.

Asked if it had any peculiarity, he replied that it was lighter on the trigger than weapons usually asked for in this country; the weapon for an expert with pistols, he added. The ordinary buyer would be afraid of a gun that went off so easily. He agreed that the revolver when handed to him by the police had only been loaded in one chamber. It contained an empty shell, and the fouling of the barrel suggested that only one shot had been fired.

"Which goes to confirm the medical evidence," said the Coroner. "A criminal seeking to destroy a man would not trust to a solitary shot. Everyone is aware that the revolver is a very unsatisfactory weapon when compared with a rifle or shot-gun. Even in countries like the United States of America, where their use is more common than here, we read of police marksmen firing many shots before they hit."

"It's the short barrel, and the kick," said the gunsmith.

"Precisely," said the Coroner. "Now, have we to hear anything from the occupants of houses to either side of the one where the dead man was found?"

The Inspector popped up again. "Very little, sir. To the right side, all the folk were out at the pictures; to the left the shot was heard, but not loudly. I did not think it necessary to bring the occupants of No. 49 here to say that, but they are willing to give evidence if necessary."

The Coroner shook his head. "I do not see that it will help us. Do you know anything about the man himself, Inspector?"

"We have not completed our inquiries yet, sir. The man had

obviously come from South Africa, and he appears at first to have been none too well provided with funds. He went out all day, though he did not tell his landlady where he was going. As we are in ignorance as to the means by which he got such a large sum of money, we are going into that carefully. We have circulated the numbers of the notes this morning, and shall know soon where they were paid out."

"Thank you," said the Coroner. "I think we may now consider the facts as we know them. The jury will consider what has been told them by the various witnesses, and, although they may possibly think of bringing in a verdict of *felo de se*, I urge them to consider particularly the evidence of the gunsmith, and the medical evidence too, with regard to the absence of burning or blackening of the wound. There is something to be said for the finding of accidental death, especially as we know that this man, formerly in poorish circumstances, was in possession of a large sum of money. Poverty causes depression and despair; the acquisition of comparative riches rarely leads a man to suicide of a physical kind, though moral suicide has been known to accompany suddenly acquired wealth."

He went on to give a resumé of the evidence, in a very businesslike way, and Patricia could see that he regarded the case as of a simple nature. To her mind, suicide was not to be thought of, but there was no getting away from the theory of accident. The rogue had accidentally compassed his own death at the moment when he had trumped a trick, brought off a coup worth ten thousand pounds, and was preparing to sail victoriously home.

She wakened up out of a reverie to see the jury file back into the court and hear the foreman announce that they had decided on a unanimous verdict. They found that Mr Hanaper had met his death by the accidental discharge of a weapon he had had in his hand falling to the floor.

The Coroner accepted their verdict, and finished with a little homily full of platitudes. The inquest was over, and Patricia hurried away to lunch.

"Mr Hanaper has slipped away," she said to herself, "but I am still here to be shot at. Mr Elphinstone was right. I was an utter ass to plunge into this business without experience. But admitting that won't give Mr Carey back his ten thousand pounds."

Then she reflected that it might. If she came forward and gave evidence about the transaction, and if that transaction proved to be a swindle, perhaps Peter Carey might recover his money.

"I expect they will trace the notes," said she, as she turned into a restaurant. "That means I shall have to appear anyway. But what a dud I shall look, and feel! 'Woman pioneer in finance finds herself fooled.' That is the kind of newspaper headline I shall get!"

CHAPTER 8 MRS GORES

The evening papers rushed out an account of the brief inquest, and before Patricia closed the office for the day, Hubert Gage-Chipnell called on her, with a copy of a pink sheet in his hand.

"You've seen this?" he said, after they had exchanged greetings. "The verdict on Hanaper, I mean?"

"I was there," said Patricia. "I went to hear it."

He started, stared at her, and put a question. "Surely you did not offer evidence?"

"No. I merely went there."

He looked relieved. "Good! But you heard what the police said about tracing the notes, of course. I don't really see the point of it myself, but it means that you had better tell them what you know."

She nodded. "That puzzled me too. It really does not seem to matter much who Hanaper was since he was not charged with anything."

He smiled. "The tidy minds of our police, I expect. They hate to leave loose ends. But here we are. They will have no difficulty in tracing Peter's money back to the source. You see, the poor chap, after deducting your commission and spending a bit, had most of it intact. Well, my idea is that you should go to Scotland Yard straight away. My car is below, and I'll drive you there and wait for you. Go in, tell them that Hanaper was a client of yours and vendor of an African concession, and was paid ten thousand by Peter. That will be all they will want to know, enough to establish the dead man's position more or less."

"I think you are right," she murmured. She was debating with herself if she ought to tell Hubert of her doubts, but refrained in the end. "Thank you very much. I'll go with you now. I certainly don't want to be 'featured' in the papers if I can help it."

A minute later and they were in Hubert's car speeding towards New Scotland Yard. Patricia alighted there with some trepidation, and was civilly challenged by an officer, to whom she mentioned her business. He took her into the building, showed her into an office, and asked her to wait. In two minutes a large, close-shaven man, with brooding grey eyes, entered and greeted her.

"You are Miss Repton, and you have come about that Willesden business?" he asked.

"Yes. Of course I know nothing about the affair itself. I merely came to explain about the money found in the dead man's room."

"I am glad you came," he said slowly. "We like to know who our suicides are, especially when there are any circumstances connected with a case that are of interest to us."

Patricia nodded. "Well, it is quite a simple matter. Mr Hanaper came to me to ask me to negotiate an African mining concession for him. I was fortunate in finding a purchaser, and the business went through at once. Mr Peter Carey was the buyer, and he gave Mr Hanaper a cheque for ten thousand pounds. My commission was deducted. The sum the police found was round about the balance, allowing for Mr Hanaper having spent a little."

The large man permitted a small smile to relieve the gravity of his lips.

"Did you know anything of Mr Carey before he came to you?"

"No. I am a sort of finance broker, but I have just set up. I looked through the papers in connection with the concession, and they seemed all right. Mr Gage-Chipnell did the same for his cousin."

"Whose cousin, may I ask?"

"Mr Carey is Mr Gage-Chipnell's cousin. The latter is a solicitor. He does not attend to his cousin's legal business, but was asked as a favour to go through these papers."

"Did Mr Carey or his cousin know anything of Mr Hanaper?"

"No; nothing at all. But buyers do not always know sellers in a business deal."

"More's the pity," said the large man quietly. "One of our officers has an idea he has seen Mr Hanaper before."

"Where?" cried Patricia, horrified.

"Two years ago in a café in the Strand," said the official. "It appears that a gentleman from America was coming over to see the Pope, to give him a million dollars for the poor of Rome. Mr Hanaper happened to meet him, and agreed to give him ten thousand pounds (a favourite sum with him, you will notice) as a guarantee of good faith, so that he might be permitted to join in the pilgrimage. There was no harm in that, except for the fact that another man from America was induced to do the same, and failed to find the first philanthropist *or* Mr Hanaper, when he looked about for them."

"The confidence trick!" said Patricia, hanging her head.

He nodded. "The good old rule, the simple plan, Miss Repton! Hanaper was known as Williams then, and our people got both him and Trevor, who was the million-dollar giver. Trevor got eighteen months, Williams, or Hanaper, got off. Trevor stuck to it that he had tried to string both of them, not only one."

"You think that was true?"

"No, I don't. Now, Miss Repton, I am sorry for you, since this concession has all the appearance of a stumer. I hope this Mr Carey will not try to take you to law about it—he might allege negligence or something."

She shook her head. "I am sure he will not. But I am thoroughly ashamed of myself. I don't see what I could have done, but I do feel that a business agent should not let people in like that."

He smiled. "You are not the first. The biggest men in business make bloomers sometimes. The swindled American I told you of was a Cincinnati lawyer. So you err in good company."

Patricia shook her head. "What an ass I shall look when this gets into the papers."

He looked at her in a kindly way. "Is there any reason why it should? Hanaper is dead, and his misdeeds with him. We are not concerned with him any longer. Of course, if Mr Carey wants his money back, he will have to prove it was his, or if he decides to take you to law, we can't help it. But you know better about that than I."

She reflected ruefully for a moment. "Mr Carey knows me, and visits my friends. I am sure he will take no action."

"Then we can't act without him. It would be necessary for him to swear any information. So you are all right."

"Far from it," said poor Patricia. "If Mr Carey does nothing to get his money back, I have let him in for a loss of ten thousand pounds! How can I repay him? If I were in a position to do so, I should not be in business. The fact that he is a wealthy man does not help me much."

"It does, Miss Repton, since that is the only kind of man who can afford to lose ten thousand and take no action. But I see what you mean. Now, wait a moment; did you not see any flaw in the documents relating to the concession? What was your authority for thinking the place had any mining value?"

"A report from a well-known mining engineer—Mr Gores."

"Then go to see him. Ask him candidly if there is anything in it."

"But he is dead."

The official smiled in spite of himself. "Dead men make excellent witnesses for rogues, Miss Repton. They can't be called in court."

Patricia rose. "Thank you for the suggestion at least. If you want me again, you can ring me up at my office in Queen Street. I hope it won't be necessary."

"I hope not," he said, getting up to let her out. "If you will let me advise you, you will see Mr Carey, tell him what I have told you, and hear what he says. Personally, I think Hanaper might have made a fool of a much more experienced financier than you. At all events, let me thank you for coming."

He had been helpful and kind. Patricia told herself as she went back to Hubert and the car. Her first impulse was to tell Hubert what she had heard, but it is hard to admit that one has perpetrated a folly, and she had felt when she met him that Gage-Chipnell was rather sceptical about her capabilities as a business-woman, even if he liked her in a social capacity.

Her mention of Tom Gores, the mining engineer, had also brought that unfortunate man back to her mind. He was beyond her reach, but perhaps he had left some relation, a widow, or a son, or daughter, who might know something. It was only natural that poor Patricia should grasp at a straw to save her reputation for intelligence.

"Well, what luck?" asked Hubert, as she got into the car and they set off for her home, "Did that satisfy them?"

"Oh, quite," said she truthfully. "They only wanted to know how he had come by that money."

She gasped a little as she said that, for now she would have to ask Peter Carey not to tell his cousin of her folly. Hubert nodded.

"I thought so. If they went into the past history of every suicide, they would have no time for any other work."

He dropped her at the door of the flat, hoped that he would see her again soon at the Elphinstones', and drove off. Patricia went into the flat, made some tea, drank it quickly, and then bolted to the nearest Public Library.

"If any of the Gores are left, they may be in a boarding-house— in which case the directory won't give them, and I shall have to enquire at the Association of Mining Engineers, or whatever it is called," she mused, as she entered the reference room, and took up the London Directory. "Or perhaps they have gone abroad, or retired into the country."

She found no less than three people of that name in the London or suburban area. One lived near the Vale of Health, Hampstead, and as she was a "Mrs Gores" Patricia decide to call on her first. No time was to be lost, since she would have to see

Peter Carey soon, but it might be wise to wait until eight o'clock, in case Mrs Gores dined late. Seven would be about the suburban hour for that meal.

She left again, and went to a restaurant to dine. At half past seven she was on her way to Hampstead, and a quarter to eight found her toiling up the steep of Fitzjohn's Avenue.

Mr Gores had been a prominent man in his day, but the little house near the Vale of Health did not suggest that he had left his widow in the lap of luxury. It was a rather dingy little two-storied place, with a small garden.

Patricia entered the gate and rang a bell. The door was opened by a servant, unexpectedly well dressed, and not ill-spoken.

Patricia asked if she might see Mrs Gores for a moment, and handed over her card. She was shown into a drawing-room which was small but well furnished, full of African souvenirs of small size; ivory carvings, native bead-work, fine Buganda grass-work, and photographs of tropical scenes. Patricia felt happy at the sight of them. She had hit on the right person, it seemed.

The lady who entered presently was a small but wiry woman, almost handsome, about thirty-three, and dressed in a frock that was not by any means new, but had obviously come from an expensive place. Patricia liked the look of her, her good-humoured mouth, her steady eyes. Her voice when she greeted her visitor was cultured, a rather husky voice though.

"I understand that you wish to see me, Miss Repton?" she said, glancing at the card she held in her hand.

"I must apologise for coming so late," said Patricia. "I really have some business of importance, or I should not have troubled you."

"I am sure you would not," said the lady who had taken Patricia in at a glance. "I don't mean, of course to suggest that you are troubling me now! Won't you sit down, and let me hear what it is?"

They both sat. Patricia hesitated for a moment, then began: "I have recently started in the City as a sort of financial agent, and a proposition was brought to me the other day which I agreed to offer. It related to an African mining concession."

Mrs Gores sat up very straight, and her eyes were fixed keenly on her visitor. "Ah, I see. You are aware that my husband was a mining engineer."

Patricia could see that she was much moved, though a high courage kept the tears back. She hurried on, "Yes. To make a long story short, I sold this concession. The sum of ten thousand pounds was paid over, and there were to be contingent mining royalties, if the area proved metalliferous and was exploited by the purchaser."

"Naturally."

"The vendor, however, was found dead the other day. His name was Hanaper, and the verdict was suicide."

Mrs Gores started. "Good Heavens, Miss Repton! I saw it in the evening paper.—Was that the man?"

Patricia nodded. "Yes. But now let me get closer to my trouble in the matter. When I examined the papers connected with the deal, I was largely influenced by seeing your late husband's name there. He had reported favourably. I looked him up in a book of reference and saw his high qualifications."

Mrs Gores' eyes were snapping now. "Was this near a place called Bangele?"

"It was. Do you know it?"

Mrs Gores did not answer the question. "What did you say the name was—Oh, I remember, the man in the paper—Hanaper."

Patricia was flushed with excitement now. "Why do you ask?"

Mrs Gores rose. She, too, was excited and flushed, and her mouth twitched a little at the corners. She put a handkerchief for a moment to her eyes, then recovered herself.

"Will you excuse me for a moment, Miss Repton? I think I have something to show you that will explain a good deal. I am more than glad you came."

Patricia nodded, and watched her hostess go out. Her excitement grew almost unbearable. Mrs Gores knew Bangele. There was such a place after all which had been visited by her dead husband. She waited most impatiently for the widow's return. What would she have to show her? What new revelation was she to have on the business affair which had begun so prosaically in her Queen Street office?

CHAPTER 9 ONE
OR THE OTHER

When Mrs Gores returned to the room, Patricia detected tears in her eyes, and promptly dropped her own to the packet of letters the other woman held in her hand.

This was tied with fresh blue ribbon, a bundle of perhaps twenty bulky envelopes. Mrs Gores sat down near her, and untied the packet, beginning to sort the letters out by the dates on the envelopes, until she withdrew two, and put the remainder on a table.

"These were from my husband," she said, composed again, and meeting Patricia's eyes directly. "I shall read you one or two passages that seem to have a bearing on what you have told me."

Patricia knew that the reading must be a strain on her companion; in a sense, a reopening of a hardly healed wound.

"You are very good," she said. "I am afraid I am worrying you rather."

Mrs Gores did not reply. She had found a place in one of the letters, and began to read in a clear and steady voice.

"You will be interested to hear that I have made Bangele after a rather trying trip. One of the totos was killed by a leopard and he was that bright little chap you liked so much. Then we came through Ungoto when the crops had failed, and were hard put to it to get enough scoff for our crowd. But here we are, and the Chief professes to like me. We had a big shauri, and I am at liberty to look round. My experience tells me that there are possibilities here. Lepper says so

67

too, but I don't think he knows anything about it."

"Who was Lepper?" asked Patricia, as Mrs Gores paused.

"That I don't know. I mean, I don't know much about him. In an earlier letter Tom speaks of having picked up a white on the way. He found him stuck in a native village, where he had made free with a native's cultivated patch, and was in danger of being speared for it. That must be Lepper."

"You have been out there?" asked Patricia, as Mrs Gores turned to the next letter.

"Twice," said the little lady, nodding. "This last time I did not go."

There was a world of regret in her voice, and Patricia said no more. Mrs Gores read again.

"As I told you in my last, I was very hopeful. Now I have made a report. I think very favourably of the whole thing, and I believe it will be one of the best, if it can be got going. Lepper is very helpful after all, though he is not an experienced man in these parts. But he is shrewd and clever. Now, my idea is this: I get back to the coast as soon as I can, and mail a copy of my report to a Belgian I know. His people may take it up, or he may put me on to some other crowd. It will take big money, and time, but I feel it will repay all. (Later.) I hear the AC, Mr Pulter, is on his way up here. A good man for the job, I believe, and can make things regular. He only gets as far as this once in nine months, but seems to have made an impression on 'Old Fishbones', as I call the Chief.—I'll explain that joke when I come home."

Mrs Gores paused, turned a page or two and looked at Patricia. "He resumes a week later—this is the last I got from him. Here is what he says: *Well, all seems to be clear. Pulter most helpful. Old Fishbones brought up to scratch too. You might buy one of those compendious pocket-knives for me, and mail at once. It's for him. Let it have plenty of buttonhooks, pickers, scissors, and other gadgets on it. I think I might let Lepper in on this, He has been useful in many ways.—I was just about to fasten this up when the saddest news came in. Pulter was about five miles on his way home, and walked into some dam fool's elephant-trap. You know the sort. I went out at once to bring him in, but it's no go. A beastly sight. He was a good fellow . . ."*

Mrs Gores' lips quivered. She stopped abruptly. Patricia bit her lip and remained silent.

"That was the last," said Mrs Gores, with an effort. "I have heard no more. The report was not mailed, for poor Tom never reached the coast."

Patricia with a shudder remembered the dictum of the Scotland Yard official, "Dead men are good witnesses for rogues." The other witness was dead too. She spoke after a moment.

"There is no mention of anyone called Hanaper."

"There is this man Lepper," said Mrs Gores, and her eyes were suddenly fierce.

Patricia nodded. "I wonder was it Hanaper?"

The other set her teeth. "I hope it was Hanaper. I hope the brute got what he deserved when that pistol went off."

"But was there any question about your husband having— been killed by a wounded buffalo?"

"I don't know. I do know that, if you have my husband's report on this place, then Lepper (or Hanaper) stole it. A man who steals like that might be a murderer too."

"But it was his name that figured in the concession."

Patricia stopped when she had said that. She remembered the forged note in the margin of the document. If Hanaper was a forger, anything was possible. But was that a forged note? She also remembered now that de Villegaile had denied even knowing the name Hanaper when she had first telephoned to him, though he produced a letter from the latter on the occasion of her visit.

"That is the difficulty," said Mrs Gores, with a sigh. "I can't understand that. You know from my husband's letter that he talked as if the concession were his own. I wonder if it lapsed, and was taken up after by this other man, Hanaper?"

"No," said Patricia. "Mr Pulter's name figured in it. Mr Pulter died before your husband. Hateful as the idea is, I think the man called Lepper was really Hanaper; at least the man I knew by that name."

"It is an extraordinary position, Miss Repton."

"It is. I was beginning to wonder if my client, or rather my friend Mr Carey, had bought the concession that did not exist. Now it is obvious that he bought something of potential value."

"*If* he could buy something when the title to it is doubtful," said Mrs Gores, though not sharply. "My husband discovered this place, and it was his knowledge that made it valuable."

"Legally I don't think you could claim, unless you could prove that the documents were forged," said Patricia. "But Mr Carey is the last man in the world to stand on a legal quibble. At the same time, I can't forget that he paid ten thousand for what appeared to be the property of the vendor."

"My dear Miss Repton, I don't feel inclined to forget that fact either. But I am in an awkward position. My husband was often the servant of others, and what he made on his own account he spent in trying to find a mining area for himself. My means are small, and there is a mortgage on this house. I shall not attempt to interfere with Mr Carey, but I think I must consult someone. If there was any crookedness about this thing, it ought to be enquired into."

"Absolutely," said Patricia. "Mr Carey will be the first to say so. I'll put your point of view before him."

Mrs Gores smiled. "You can be quite sure that I should not allow Mr Carey to lose his money, even if I could prove that the concession had been granted to my husband. That ten thousand would be the first charge on any profits."

Patricia had taken to her from the first. "I expected that of you," she said warmly, "But now we are in this position. Mr Carey is the owner, so far as we know. How are you going to decide if the vendor had no real title to sell? Mr Pulter is dead, Hanaper (if he is really the Lepper of your husband's letters) is dead."

"I shall go out," said Mrs Gores, as decidedly as if she had made up her mind long ago. "Poor Tom is buried out there. I could not go even to visit his grave as things stood. But, if there is a chance of my proving that this concession is now mine, I can chance it."

"Why, it's in the interior!" cried Patricia, "I think it a plucky idea, but is it wise?"

Mrs Gores shrugged. "My dear, I, frankly, have not quite enough to live on, and I am one of those unfortunate women who know no trade, and have no profitable accomplishments. If I sell out here, pay off the mortgage, and auction some of my furniture, I shall have about fifteen hundred left. That will be just enough."

"It seems a frightful gamble," cried Patricia, "It may not be so bad for you, since you have been there before, but what if you fail? You will have lost all you have."

"What is it but a gamble now?" asked the other. "To try to live on paying-guests in a house that is not big enough, to know that every half year the interest on the mortgage is due, and wonder if you can meet it: that is a gamble, but there are no winnings."

"Will you see Mr Carey first?" said Patricia. "I wish you would. I am rather in a hole myself with regard to him, for I sold the thing, and I hate eating humble pie."

"I know," said Mrs Gores. "It is the body of at least one meal a day for me. Miss Repton, if you knew how I hate it! If you knew how, silly as it may seem, even the prospect of getting into the sun by myself, wandering where I will, being my own mistress, looks gorgeous, a dream! I always felt well out there. I never had fever. Tom said I was a wonder. Here I am never really well. I mope, and the cold tries me a great deal. If someone came along and told you that there was possibly a mine of riches waiting for you in the blue, wouldn't you go?"

Patricia nodded. "You make it sound very interesting. I think I should feel like you. But do make sure before you decide. Mr Carey has all the documents. He would let you see them. You could make extracts from the letters you have and let him see them. If there is any possible flaw, he will only be too pleased to help."

"Why are you so sure of him?" asked the other woman.

"Because—well, because he is a boy; a nice boy. He doesn't look that, and he is quite twenty-five, but you can't get away from it once he opens his mouth. Mr Hanaper said he would take less at first, just to get the money, but Mr Carey would not hear of it. He was sorry for the man, and he insisted on giving the full sum he had asked."

"How like my poor Tom! He was the hardest headed man in the world in his own line, and one of the cleverest, but so generous and simple with money. No one could trick him on a technical point, but they had only to get on his soft side in other matters to get his last shirt.—I like your Mr Carey without seeing him."

Patricia smiled. "There are one or two other things I will tell you when we have a conference together. I must see him first and put the whole affair before him. But it won't do any harm if I tell you that I think you may be right."

"You mean that Mr Carey was tricked?"

"And myself most of all. That is what I do mean, but I can't explain now."

Mrs Gores beamed. "Will you help me unravel this? It was you who brought the news. I, at least, am not afraid to put my affair in your hands."

Patricia grimaced. "No, perhaps not, but I am afraid to take anyone's affairs now. I muddled the last."

"We are not sure yet."

"No, that is true. However, Mr Carey must really be my first charge. I owe it to him to do what I can."

Mrs Gores nodded. "I don't want you to do anything against your client—your friend. I do mean that you shan't suffer if your news brings me fortune."

"Thank you," said Patricia. "But I think I shall have to retire from business."

"I am sure you won't. You don't like cowardly people. I am sure of that. And you won't set a bad example.—Cold feet are contagious."

"You're right," laughed Patricia. "Men don't go out of business after one mistake."

"Few of them would be in business now if they did," said Mrs Gores, smiling. "Then I will see Mr Carey, if you can arrange it. And I am awfully grateful to you for coming to tell me what you have done."

"I didn't come to tell you. That is my horrible honesty. I came hoping to prove that Mr Carey was the rightful owner of the concession. But I shall see Mr Carey tomorrow and ask him to make an appointment. Would you mind coming to my office at Queen Street?"

"I will meet him anywhere. By the way, do let me get you something; some coffee?"

"Nothing, thanks," said Patricia. "I must really get home to think things over. You have my card, and you can rely on my letting you know, the moment I have fixed up an appointment with Mr Carey."

They talked for a few minutes longer, then Patricia left the house and hurried to the tube station.

She felt very tired as she sat down in the train. Far from scoring a point by her visit to Hampstead she had almost proved to herself that Mr Hanaper was a rogue of many aliases, and poor Peter Carey the buyer of a property to which he had no real title.

It all fitted in together. Hanaper's attachment to Gores' safari. Gores' softness and simplicity in matters outside his technical radius, the arrival at Bangele, and the obvious fact that the Chief was dealing with Gores direct. Then there was the evidence of Scotland Yard that Hanaper was a confidence-trickster, the inference to be drawn from the half-erased note on the document, the fact that the only valuable witnesses to the transaction were dead.

"There is still the chief—'Old Fishbones' as Gores called him," Patricia said to herself as she prepared to get out. "I suppose Mrs Gores hopes to get hold of him. But I had better wait until she and I have our chat with Peter Carey."

CHAPTER 10 PETER WAKES UP

Patricia was waiting for Peter Carey in her office. She looked worried; she was conscious that she might have a bad quarter of an hour before her, or at least deserved it, and she had, with a wholly unconscious coquetry, done her best to look pretty.

Peter, surprised into a look of open admiration, when he came in, had no idea that she was worried. He thought how jolly she looked, how stunning her hair was, what an ass he had been to decide to see the world outside before he had exploited the possibilities of the world inside. So he was doubly surprised when Patricia made him sit down, and held up her hands, the palms toward him.

"Kamerad!" she said ruefully. "You have a crow to pluck with me, and you don't know it. The irony of the thing is that I have to produce the bird myself."

Peter laughed. "I'm quite sure you are wrong, Miss Repton. I ought to know, oughtn't I?"

"You are in the position of many people," she remarked, offering him a cigarette. "You ought, but you don't—yet."

"Are you serious?" He smiled.

"Yes, this is a business talk," she said. "It appears that I have not only warmed a serpent in my bosom, but handed it on to you."

"But it hasn't stung me," he protested.

"Yes, it has," said Patricia. "Seriously, Mr Carey, I have grave

74

fears that Mr Hanaper was a rogue, and that I helped him—unwittingly of course—to sell you a pup."

He sat up now. She had known from the first that he was a man who had some character behind his boyishness.

"How did you learn this?" he asked. "The man is dead. How could you know?"

She shrugged. "I have made inquiries. At your cousin's suggestion I went to the police and told them of the deal. I was told there that Hanaper had been recognised as a confidence trickster—though he was acquitted on trial—and that tells its own tale. He tricked me, and I let him trick you. You can't know how sorry I am."

Peter's chin went out a little. "Wait a moment. Don't let's mix things. Hanaper may be what you say—though the acquittal leaves a loophole, but that does not say my concession is valueless. Can you say that it is?"

"No, I can't," she murmured. "My trouble is that I can't say if it is yours now."

He looked at her steadily. "Have you told Hubert this?"

"No. I have told him nothing. When I heard that, I made a desperate effort to save my face. I started enquiries, and they made things worse. If you don't mind, I will tell you all I know."

He nodded. "If you please. This won't ruin me, but I hate to be done."

She told him briefly all about it, about the note on the margin, M de Villegaile's denial, her visit to Mrs Gores, and that lady's surprising revelation.

He listened quietly. "As to the Belgian's denial that he knew of this Hanaper," he said, "I don't think there is much in that. He was frank enough when he saw you. He may not have liked to have someone prying into his affairs over the telephone. But Mrs Gores' story sounds ugly for us. It's circumstantial.

"It upsets us altogether," he added. "If Hanaper was also Lepper, he was only a hanger-on. He had no right to the thing. It certainly seems as if she were right; that her husband was the concessionaire, but I shan't accept that without proof. I don't

75

blame her. If I did, I should have to blame myself, and also Hubert, who is a lawyer. If this ten thousand had gone to Mrs Gores, whatever the circumstances, I don't know that I should have done anything. But I shall, as the thing stands."

"You are quite right," she said. "I advise you to approach the police, give an account of the whole affair, and claim the balance."

Peter knew very well what was passing through her mind, and he admired her moral courage in giving him the advice she hated to give. If this were brought into court it would be a sad shock to her business reputation, giving the Philistines to mock. Generously he shook his head.

"My dear Miss Repton, I have been an ass, but I like to keep it to myself. I shall not take that step."

"The trouble started in my stable," mourned Patricia. "I am the champion ass, Mr Carey."

"In any case," said he, grinning a little, "we won't compete for the title (which I am sure is justly mine), but think what we can do."

"I can begin by apologising."

"Let it finish there, please.—There remains the only witness to this transaction, the chief who gave the concession. I know nothing about Africa. I had an idea that even chiefs were gentlemen with a defective education. But this one *signed*."

"I suppose some of them go to Mission Schools," said she. "However, do go on."

"Well, I have arranged to go out. I have sent on Townard. I gave him five hundred for first expenses. Am I going to throw that away? I presume he could sue me for breach of contract if I backed out. If he did, I should have to explain matters, and it would be easier to go to the police now."

"You're generous," she murmured. "I know you are just doing this to save my face."

He laughed. "Not a bit of it. My idea is to go out as if nothing had happened, see this Negro gentleman, and learn exactly to whom the land was granted. If it was to Mr Gores, then I have nothing to say. But if it was not Mr Gores, then I shall assume myself to be the owner."

"Will you meet Mrs Gores here?

"I'd like to. Her story seems sound, but I shan't take anything for granted after this. If Hanaper was a subtle enough rogue to write in a sentence, and half erase it, so that it might seem the proposition had been offered elsewhere, he might have worked up another scheme to get my money, and then disclose a nominee as the real owner."

"I am sure Mrs Gores is quite honest," she said, finding that the Peter of her first knowledge had another side to him.

"Very likely," said he, smiling. "But it won't do any harm to enquire. What does she propose to do about it?"

"To do like you; go out and see the Chief."

"Alone?"

"She knows the country, has travelled twice there with her late husband."

"That does suggest she thinks she is right," he mused.

"Absolutely. She is going to sell up and stake her money on the chance."

"That's foolish," he said. "What will be left if she fails?"

"Very little—if anything."

He looked at her thoughtfully. "I don't like that. I must see her."

"I can get her for this afternoon. Will you come back about three?"

Peter rose. "Yes, I will. I'll have a talk to Hubert first though."

"Please not," said Patricia, flushing. "I had rather you did not until we have had this interview."

He looked at her quickly. A jealous twinge made itself felt. She had seen a lot of Hubert. Was it possible that, while she did not mind exposing her slip to him, she valued Hubert's opinion of her too highly to give herself away?

"All right," he agreed. "But don't blame yourself at all. I have heard of quite respectable pawnbrokers being saddled with stolen goods. I don't see what you could have done to safeguard

77

me."

"It is good of you to say so," said Patricia, giving him her hand. "At three then."

"I won't forget," he said, and went out.

Patricia wired to Mrs Gores, and sat down to think. She wondered if the thoughtful look which had come into Peter's eyes when he heard Mrs Gores proposed to go out alone, meant that he had an idea of joining forces. It would save Mrs Gores money, it would be an excellent idea for the two claimants to appear together, and have the matter decided in their joint presence. But was Mrs Gores sufficiently unconventional to go out with a solitary man? For the moment, she had forgotten Townard.

"It would be just like him," she said. "And Mrs Gores might do much worse."

Peter had been right in that. It would be a terrible thing if the widow put her all into the throw and lost. Suppose the title to the concession had been Gores'. Suppose, it had lapsed on his death. Suppose!

Here she checked herself. Actually Mrs Gores had not a leg to stand on! Hanaper, forger or thief, had undoubtedly destroyed the original document, if there had been one. She had no documentary evidence that her husband was the concessionaire at any time.

Mrs Gores came in a little before three, her papers in her bag. She looked tired and almost hysterical, but she pulled herself together when Peter Carey came in and was introduced to her. Then the three sat down, and Patricia began.

"Now, Mr Carey, since you left, I have thought of something. The document you have may be a forgery and worthless, but Mrs Gores has no document of any kind, except the letter which she will presently show you. That only proves things inferentially."

Peter had been studying Mrs Gores since he came in, and he smiled at her now, and then at Patricia.

"We're none of us in the law," said he, "so let's forget it. Mrs Gores and I are not litigious, I think. We want a square deal and we want to be fair. Isn't that right, Mrs Gores?"

Her tired face lighted up. "That is all I want," she said.

"And that is all Miss Repton wants," he remarked. "Only she has to appear businesslike for my sake. Now, I don't think that anything is to be learned about the matter on this side. In fact I am sure our clue lies in Africa. So I propose to go there to find out. If Mrs Gores is right, I shan't let the absence of a document stand in my way. I shall transfer whatever apparent rights I have to her, and if it is not brought into court, the document I have may serve for a title. On the other hand, if she is wrong, and I am owner, then I must remember that her husband made a long and expensive survey of the ground. I shall hope to make use of that, and pay a proper sum for the service rendered. How does that strike you, Mrs Gores?"

"I shan't ask for that if I am wrong."

"Perhaps not, but I wouldn't care to stand in anyone's debt. May I see the marked portion of the letters you received from Mr Gores?"

She opened her bag, and handed them over. He read the passages twice, and smiled again.

"On the face of it it looks as if I had thrown my money away. But I was equally convinced by the papers Hanaper put in. I hope to carry out my plans in any case. The only thing I propose to add to them is a suggestion."

Patricia's admiration rose as she sat there and watched his quiet face, the kindly smile that hovered on his lips as he looked at Mrs Gores.

"May I hear it?" asked the widow softly.

He nodded. "I have sent on a man to make arrangements for the journey up country. I understand that the cost of a safari is no light one."

"It is very costly," she said.

"Well, it seems to me ridiculous to have two expeditions when one would serve. My porters could carry your baggage, and we are not two rascally adventurers racing to get in first with a bribe to the Chief."

Mrs Gores laughed. "No. But you are putting it in this way to save my money, and also——"

Peter lifted his hand. "Just a moment. Don't imagine that I am a philanthropist because Hanaper managed to touch me for ten thousand. You will have to pay your footing, you know. I thought two hundred and fifty might be the fare."

"I don't know if you are aware of it, but your safari will cost thousands," she cried.

"I do know that. I have been sitting at the feet of Mr Townard, Mrs Gores. But you won't have all the porters, or even half. About ten will be your share, so the sum I name is fair enough."

Both women laughed. Peter grinned a little. "Or perhaps you are afraid to come with us?" he added.

She smiled a little. "I once travelled nine hundred miles to join my husband, in charge of a one-eyed Somali, who turned out afterwards to be a former follower of the Somali Mad Mullah. No, I am not afraid. But I know enough of conditions out there to understand that your offer is a most generous one."

Peter laughed. "I didn't come here to blush, but to do business. The question is, do you care to accept the offer? I am quite serious about it, if you are serious about going."

"I ought not to take advantage of your kindness."

"If I met you on a mountain in a snowstorm, I suppose you wouldn't allow me to guide you, or help you out?"

"Of course I should, but——"

"And I suppose that part of Africa is about as dangerous?"

"Oh, more. But you see——"

"Then I think you will be wise to accept," he said. "But think it over." He turned to Patricia. "You have no objection to my consulting Hubert now?"

She bit her lip. "How can I? After all, I think you are right to put it before him."

When he had gone, Mrs Gores turned to Patricia. "What a charming fellow," she said enthusiastically. "He's wonderfully generous. He does remind me of poor Tom in that. I am sure I shall like him tremendously."

Patricia looked at her. Yes, she was handsome, and now she was animated too. Something seemed to sting her. She could not say what it was; an extraordinary sensation, flashing on the brain for a moment, searing in its swift passage.

"I think so too," she said, uncomfortably.

CHAPTER 11
HUBERT SPEAKS

Though she could not explain why she cared less that Peter Carey should know of her mistake than his cousin Hubert, the fact remained that it was so. Hubert was not financially interested in the affair, Peter was, but then she knew that Hubert was neither boyish nor youthful like his cousin, and when he came into her office next day alone, she felt, for the first time in her life, positively shy.

Hubert was smiling faintly, and she wondered if she ought to hate him for that, or if it was only an attempt on his part to put her at her ease.

"Well, you've heard all about the great bloomer now," she said, as she shook hands, and made him sit down. "What do you think of it?"

Hubert bowed his head in mock humility. "What do I think of myself, you mean? You are new to business, Peter is a fledgling in the world, but I am supposed to be a lawyer and a man of affairs. My dear Miss Repton, don't hesitate to put the blame on the right head—in this instance mine. What is a lawyer for but to keep his clients out of trouble? And I have lamentably failed."

Put that way, it sounded credible. He was a lawyer, and he was familiar with documents of all kinds, including those most complex things of all, human documents. Patricia began to feel that she was not the only blameworthy person in the world.

"Then we all shared in it," she said. "I thought you would be full of legal indignation."

"Not an indig in me," said he. "It does not behove the pot to blacken the character of the kettle. But this discloses a nice state of affairs."

She nodded. "You have heard what your cousin proposes to do," she said. "I think he is acting most generously."

"Which in this case means most idiotically," said Hubert. "Please don't exclaim! I am now talking as a lawyer who failed once at his job and means never to give extra-legal advice again."

"Then you don't think he is right?" she said, in surprise.

"I am sure he isn't. We don't know anything about Lepper's relations with Gores, we don't know that he was the man we knew as Hanaper. There is not the slightest proof of it. Then Mrs Gores received a letter from her husband some time before his death. She doesn't know what may have happened in the interim."

"What could have happened?"

"With the death of the concessionaire the concession may have lapsed. Or Hanaper may have been out there and bought it from Gores—even if he was not the man who called himself Lepper."

"But we hear he was suspected of being a confidence trickster. He may have been or he may not. Even if he was, he might have invested his ill-gotten gains in this. I can conceive of a burglar buying a motor out of the money he got by stealing. If he sold it second-hand it would still be an honest car; and if you paid him for it, it would be a respectable and honest transaction. I am only suggesting, of course, that Peter may have bought some real property from a man who, whatever his former character, had a real title to it. Mrs Gores has no title that she can show. Her husband's letter, as quoted to me by Peter, refers to the matter solely by inference."

"That is quite true," said Patricia, somewhat disturbed in her mind. "But surely the Chief can prove it?"

"If he is alive he may. Even then he could not say if——"

"Oh, yes, he could," cried Patricia triumphantly. "You see, there were two men, Hanaper and Gores. Even if Mr Gores agreed to cede the concession to the other, the Chief would know it."

"I withdraw that," said Hubert gracefully. "You are quite right. But, as a lawyer, I insist on Peter's not compromising his position in advance by admitting the possibility of this other claim. It's most unwise."

"But they will arrive at the same time, and they will both hear the Chief's evidence as to the buyer."

"I object to that! Look here, Miss Repton, you know something of Peter now. What would you say of his character?"

"He is extremely generous."

"And extremely susceptible," said Hubert, with a laugh. "I put it to you that his going out with that lady is foolish beyond belief. He told me something of her yesterday, and he said she was not at all old, but seemed a very nice little woman."

Patricia smiled. "So she is."

His smile broadened. "When a fellow of Peter's temperament begins with 'nice little woman', he proceeds by degrees to 'charming little woman,' 'fascinating little woman' and finally 'little woman' itself, a phrase which is much more tender and intimate than it is when qualified by any adjective."

"You seem to know," she said, twinkling.

"I hear it," he replied. "But try to look at it as everyone else will. Here is a charming little widow, who even impresses another woman with her agreeableness. A man like Peter might take to her even in London, when he would see her intermittently. What will happen if he does as he proposes, is in a position where, practically alone, he sees her every day from morning to night?"

"I know what you mean. But she is devoted to her husband's memory," said Patricia.

He laughed. "It's possible. We don't know. We do know that, even if there was no question of a concession to be gained, Mrs Gore would make a hit if she caught Peter."

"She doesn't really know who he is."

"That I can't say. But she knows that a man who can throw

away ten thousand without wanting to go to law to recover it; a man who can afford to be so generous that he takes her for nothing practically while he pays for the expenses of the safari, is a very eligible party."

"She might not care for him like that."

"Did she say so?"

Patricia smiled. Mrs Gores had not said so. She felt that Hubert might be in the right. She knew next to nothing of Mrs Gores. Peter prided himself on judging by people's faces. He had not been very successful with Mr Hanaper.

"I suppose you told him what you thought?" she said.

"Vigorously but tersely, you bet! Also I made no impression. Peter's chin went out, and for a moment I thought he was going to say something about lawyers in my old uncle's best manner. But he only said that he had your backing."

Patricia bit her lip. She had certainly approved of what Peter had offered, and said so.

"Well, I thought it generous."

"So do I. But Peter's virtues run to excess—they only step over the borderland into sinful folly. Another thing: Peter is a landowner and a man of position in his county. He likes the place and will ultimately live in it when this African fever is over. Now you know something of the country, and what will be said when it is known down there that Peter has gone into the wilds with a widow?"

"It need not be known."

"No, but it will. If Peter was to espouse a native lady in darkest Africa it would be all over the village within a month. There is nothing hid when the county gets on the ramp."

She laughed. "Well, what can I do? Unsay what I have said?"

"Take your hand from the plough and turn back? No. By no means. But what about the lady herself? If she is the sorrowing phoenix you believe her to be, why not approach her again, gently let fall the suggestion that people may talk, and disclose Peter's position at home as that of an influential man whose aristocratic career may be ruined by a scandal. If she is all right, and has no designs on our poor Peter, she will find a way to back out, and so preserve her reputation, and his. If she prefers to go on, we shall know that she flies at high game."

Patricia shook her head. "No, I can't do that. It seems to me that it will end by my going out with them as chaperon. What about that?"

He looked at her hard. "You aren't serious?"

She composed her face. "Why not?"

"It's preposterous!" he said, almost sharply. "Why, that would be madness itself."

She burst into a laugh. "I actually managed to pull your leg! You see, she would be a chaperon for me, being a widow—I mean Mrs Gores being a widow! I shouldn't mind it a bit, but I don't think I could tack myself on to your cousin's caravan at such short notice, and with such an inadequate reason."

He relaxed again. "But you do see my point, don't you?"

"I see it, if I can't quite believe in it," she said. "I would do anything I could to make up for putting your cousin on this dubious speculation. I suppose I ought to return my commission?"

"Peter won't let you. Don't worry about that. But I really do feel now that it would not be fair to ask you to speak to Mrs Gores. I am sorry I suggested it. But what can we do? You see that I am trying to act for the best, to protect Peter from someone who may be, for all we know, what the Victorians called 'a designing female'."

"Can you protect any man from designing females?"

"I suppose not. It has been the hard but ineffectual task of loving mothers and affectionate fathers since the world began. Still, we must try.—Would you advise my having a shot at it?"

She looked at him, took a cigarette from her box, and passed it to him. "I don't see how you can. Coming from an outsider and a man, however you wrapped it up in politeness, it would be an insult. Then your cousin might resent it."

He lighted up, frowning a little. "He would. That's the rub. Peter is soft as satin till you rub the fabric the wrong way; then he can be nasty."

"Any other ideas?"

"None yet. It's the dickens of a business. Looking after Peter is like caressing a hedgehog and trying to think it great fun. But what about the heritage of your sex—intuition? Does it suggest nothing?"

"The heritage is proverbial rather than general," she said lightly. "On the whole, I think young men must be left to look after themselves."

"Some detrimental usually takes up the duty," he remarked. "But will you try to edge in a word in season if the opportunity turns up?"

"I might," she replied doubtfully.

"Do. I'll have another go at him myself."

She looked down. "Yesterday I got another glimpse of your cousin, from a new angle. He isn't as ingenuous as he looks. I think you will find that he can manage his affairs pretty well."

Hubert rose. "I hope so indeed. I am very anxious about him. He's a good sort, and so little spoils a man's career nowadays. I think a trip in Africa would harden and make a man of him, but I mean a trip alone. I don't think a woman in the camp is likely to help."

Patricia got up too, and put her cigarette in an ash-tray. "Our sex is much maligned. Some of us meet you half way, but some of you run up to us and then declare you simply stood still!"

"We are still the unfair sex," he agreed, holding out his hand. "Thanks awfully anyway for talking it over. I can rely on you to say something, if you think it will go down. My own invidious task is to play the lawyer without a heart. If I can put a stop to this nonsense I will."

Patricia smiled. "Goodbye. I don't know if I wish you luck, or not, in your task."

"On my head alone be it," he said, and went out smiling.

Patricia sat down again. She was thinking of Peter.

And then she wondered why she thought of Peter. She had seen much more of Hubert. She liked Hubert. That day he had given her another proof of his solicitude for his cousin's interest. But it was Peter's face that rose up most often in her mind, his funny little smile, and that slight outthrust of the chin when his obstinacy spurred him.

But, of course, Hubert had been wrong about Mrs Gores. The little widow had not earned his cynicism. She had been very grateful to Patricia, and was simply going out to get her own, if it could be proved her own. Patricia felt sure that, if Peter had not mentioned the latest scheme, Mrs Gores would never have thought of it.

It didn't seem to matter anyway—or did it?

CHAPTER 12 THE STIFF WINDOW

No one ever thinks of using the simile greyhound, or even foxhound, to symbolise Scotland Yard. Beagle is the hound nearest to it—the slow but pertinacious one who does not hope to overtake his hare by speed, but sticks to the trail as long as the scent holds.

That evening Patricia was surprised to receive a visit from the stout man she had seen at New Scotland Yard. He came to her little flat, and announced himself as Detective-Inspector Hoe.

Patricia made him sit down in her tiny drawing-room, and passed him the cigarettes.

"What is it now?" she asked lightly. "Surely Mr Hanaper is dead enough!"

The large man nodded. "But still rather a nuisance, miss. You see, our people have an unholy way of keeping on, and any stray bit of news that comes in from the uniformed forces is passed on to us. But we'll come to that presently. I just came to ask you how it was that Mr Hanaper came to you."

"I think I told you it was my advertisement," she said.

"So you did. What troubles me is this. A rogue might think it was an easy business to string a lady like yourself who had not set up long. My theory is that there was someone else behind that, a confederate."

Patricia smiled. "Even now, I don't quite see that it matters. Mr Carey is not taking any legal action, Hanaper is dead, and the spilt milk will be hard to collect."

"What if it was spilt blood, miss?" said Hoe.

Patricia started, and stared at him. "What a horrid way to put it! But we know what happened. The inquest made that clear enough."

The large man shook his head. "This is all in confidence, miss, and you mustn't tell anyone. But, in my opinion, the inquest may have fouled the trail instead of following it."

Her eyes were horrified. "What can that mean?"

Inspector Hoe had a matter-of-fact manner. He raised his eyebrows slightly, but did not seem at all excited. "Well, miss, you know what was said at the inquest. That was all right. On what they heard, the jury had no option but to bring in the verdict they did. The revolver was found in the room, which no one had entered, the money had not been touched, which did away with the motive of robbery. So they brought it in accident."

"Don't you agree with that?"

"I can't say. We have to examine hundreds of clues that lead to nothing, and we have theories we find incorrect; being human like the rest of the world. All I do say is that a little circumstance has been brought to our notice by a constable on a Willesden beat that gives the case a new twist."

"Oh, does it throw any new light on Hanaper's identity?"

"None, miss. He and the man who went to jail came to this country five years ago from Johannesburg. I don't know if they were native-born, or simply went out there on their peculiar business. But both were men of the same type, bearded (perhaps to make strangers think they were what used to be called Colonial types), soft-spoken, dressing in a way that did not suggest London tailoring. This new thing has nothing to do with that."

"Was the constable on the beat that took in the house where Mr Hanaper died?" she asked eagerly.

"He was. He is a very nice fellow, a superior sort of man, and well-liked locally. You know, some of the force are very efficient, and polite too, but somehow they do not invite or receive confidences. They're not always the worst sort either."

"I can imagine it."

"PC Trade, on the other hand is, I hear, the adviser of lots of people. They come to him to settle little disputes, even to ask him about legal points he doesn't understand. Well, miss, you may remember at the inquest the people owning the house to one side of the place where Hanaper lived, had closed up and gone to the pictures."

"I remember that distinctly. Have they discovered something?"

"Not knowingly. It's this way. The man of the house came to Trade yesterday. He's a draper's clerk, but he lets a room or two furnished when he can, to help out the rent."

"And he had a tenant?" began Patricia excitedly.

"No, but he had both rooms vacant when Hanaper was killed," said the Inspector mildly. "One in the 'return' similar to the one Hanaper occupied in the next house. Two evenings ago he had an offer to take one room. He agreed. The prospective tenant asked might he see the place? He took him up. You know it has been hot and the room was stuffy. He threw up the window, and then he got a shock."

Patricia leaned forward eagerly. "He found something?"

Hoe twinkled. "In a way he did. The last tenant of the room, who had left six weeks before, had complained when he was leaving that the window was stiff, and he had nearly broken his back trying to get it up. The landlord had thought of having it done, but put it off until he should hear of a new tenant. He knew the window was stiff, but when he pushed it up it ran as if oiled. There was no magic about it either. When he examined it carefully next day he found the marks of a tool, and saw how the window had been eased."

"Good gracious!" cried Patricia, "but how far was it from one return to another?"

"Good shot, miss," said Hoe. "You get my idea wonderfully. We haven't an atom of direct evidence, but it seems to me that someone got into that other house, when the occupiers were out at the pictures, fixed up the window go that it opened noiselessly, took a pot-shot at his man, then threw the pistol through the open window into the room across the way."

Patricia nodded quickly. "Yes, of course. But if he had first to fix the stiff window, he must have known that Hanaper was not in the room at the time. Hanaper had his own window open. He would have heard something."

"That's right. The odds are that the other man knew of his movements, entered the other return when Hanaper had not yet returned, and then lay for him."

"There are houses at the back," said Patricia. "If it was dark someone would have seen the Hash."

"They might, miss, on one condition, that the pistol muzzle was projecting from, or on a line with, the window. But this clerk says a chair that usually stands in a corner was about a yard from the side wall, facing the window, but well in the room. A man who would trust to shooting another in the head with a revolver must be a crack. To my mind, he knelt by the chair, well inside the room to hide the flash, rested his pistol-arm on the seat, and let fly. Then he stalked up to the window, chucked the weapon across the twenty-two feet separating the returns, and closed the window."

"But how did he get in?"

He shook his head. "Ah, there you have me."

"But why only one cartridge?"

"Perhaps to give the impression of suicide. A man holding a gun to his own head ought not to miss. Perhaps because the fellow, as I have said, was not used to wasting cartridges. But, mind you, this is all in the air. The local people are going into it, and I don't know yet what they will report. What I really came to you about is this: Did Mr Hanaper, as he called himself, talk of any pal of his; not by name necessarily?"

"He said Mr Gores was a pal of his, the engineer who surveyed the mining concession. But I don't believe that."

"No one else?"

"No. But, Inspector, you leave me rather in the dark. If you think he was killed by a confederate, what was the motive? We know the money was untouched."

Hoe nodded. "Well, there are two possibilities. He may have thought he could get into the other room and sneak the money, then found the shot had attracted too much attention."

"He might have known that."

"Oh dear, no. A good many shots have been fired in houses and have been mistaken for slamming doors, or motor exhausts. The other thing is this: Division of the loot causes more trouble between criminals than anything else. To be double-crossed, as they call it, makes them angrier than anything else. Hanaper, for all we know, may have promised his pal halves, made an attempt to collar all, and been shot in revenge. That is my idea here. He had been asked to cough up—to pay up, and refused. The other rogue couldn't sue him legally, so took the ugly way out."

Patricia shivered a little. It crossed her mind that she might tell the Inspector about her visit to Mrs Gores, and the man named Lepper. The latter might not be Hanaper after all, but the original thief of Gores's documents, who had passed them on for Hanaper to forge and negotiate.

But she did not tell Hoe. It was all conjecture so far, and Peter Carey would hate to be held up at the last moment by a reopening of the case, and legal proceedings which might after all turn out to be based on a mistaken theory. One ruffian had slain another. That was, at the worst, what it came to.

"You spoke of a client or friend of yours who paid Hanaper a large sum," he went on, as she reflected. "What is he going to do now?"

She told him, and added that as there were only two possible claimants to the concession, and both were going out together, there was no necessity to worry.

"They are both compromising to a certain extent," she said, "and I think it is wise."

"Their business isn't ours," he agreed. "But do you mean that this widow lady is going out alone with Mr Carey?"

"Yes," said Patricia, smiling. "Conventions aren't so hard and fast out there as they are here."

"They may make a match of it, and so make sure of the concession," laughed the Inspector. "Well, miss, keep this to yourself for the present. We may need your help again, and, if so, I will write or telephone you."

He rose. She detained him with a lifted hand. "Have they not found any marks in the other house to show how the man may have got in?"

"Gloves are cheap nowadays," said he, smiling. "No gentleman of the fraternity would be seen working without them."

She nodded. "But there is one thing you have overlooked, I imagine, the pistol. It was brought to that gunsmith's by Mr Hanaper himself."

Hoe was amused. "So, if I brought in your watch to get it mended, you couldn't claim it? I brought it in; so I must own it? No, miss. We don't know that Hanaper was not asked by his pal to take the thing in. As he was chosen to negotiate the papers, he must have been the less notorious of the two."

"I wonder why you tell me all this?" asked Patricia.

"Why not?" said he. "Bless you, miss, we're not half so mysterious as people make out—especially when there is no point in it. I wouldn't broadcast it to a reporter, but I know you are safe, and I know I may want your help, which you will be all the more ready to give when you know that the affair may be serious."

"Then you really like people to come forward willingly?"

"Of course we do. You wouldn't believe the crooked answers we get from quite decent people, who just want to keep out of trouble and don't care who suffers."

"Well, I am at your disposal any time," said Patricia.

When Hoe had gone, she sat down and thought it out. She, too, did not want to have trouble, or go into court, but in the circumstances she felt it was up to her not to let a consideration of that kind stand in her way. Hoe's theory sounded very solid, almost as solid as the man himself. The circumstances surrounding Hanaper's death had been so suggestive of suicide or accident that not even the police had thought of searching the adjoining house. But then, if it had not been for the clerk's prospective tenant, it might not have occurred to them to fix on the clue of the once stiff window.

She was still thinking over it when the telephone bell rang, and she heard Mrs Elphinstone's voice.

"That you, Pat?"

Patricia assented. "I wonder if you were going to ask me to come to tea tomorrow? I had made up my mind to."

Mrs Elphinstone laughed. "Intelligent anticipation. Do come! Mr Gage-Chipnell was here today, quite upset about his favourite, Peter. Have you heard of this mad idea, eloping with a widow, and so on?"

"Not of that particularly mad idea," laughed Patricia, "but I know Mr Carey intends to escort a widow to the place where her husband was buried."

"What a strange form of gaiety!" cried the old lady. "I never heard of such a thing. But we've all got to stop it. This woman will run away with him if we are not careful."

"Don't count me in as a chaperon," said Patricia. "I simply refuse. I don't wear apron-strings, even if Mr Carey wanted to knot himself to them, which he doesn't. But I'll come tomorrow with pleasure."

"I am glad," said the old lady. "Come early—before the others." And she rang off without telling Patricia who those others were.

CHAPTER 13
OBSTINACY

"Do you hate him so much?" said Mrs Elphinstone.

"No, but I like him awfully," said Patricia, smiling at her old friend. "But I must hide a breaking heart behind a—what is the right phrase?"

"A joyful countenance," said the old lady. "Pat, I think you are very foolish. It isn't as if I were one of those hard-faced people who think sentiment sloppy and romance out of date. But I don't know when I have met a young man who attracted me as much as Peter Carey, and was eligible as well—*so* eligible, my dear!"

Patricia patted her hand. "No go! I can't drape myself about his neck and beg him not to go. Besides, Mrs Gores is as respectable as you or I."

"I refuse to be called respectable!" said Mrs Elphinstone. "At my age, such an epithet is unkind. There need be no draping; on the other hand, you need not throw him into the arms of an experienced woman ten years older."

"I had no hand in the throwing. But really I see no danger. Mr Carey is generous, but he is not an ass. I couldn't put any sincerity into an attempt to queer Mrs Gores's pitch."

"You do use such odd phrases, my dear. I hope you are not referring to the pitch we are proverbially warned against?"

"I'll bring Mrs Gores to see you," Patricia suggested.

Mrs Elphinstone raised her hands in protest. "Don't! I have set my heart on this, and I will not be placated by fascinating women. Did you know I had invited Mr Carey and his cousin here today?"

"Of course I did. Your intrigues are very tortuous, you know, but they wind back to the same point. Poor Mr Carey, are we to be two women and one man against him, lecturing, advising, coaxing him, praying him to beware of the widder?"

"We are going to save him from himself," the old lady laughed. "Isn't that nice?"

"Hateful," said Patricia. "The most vicious idea of all. I shall be neutral."

Mrs Elphinstone pricked up her ears. "Someone is coming up the stairs now."

Patricia jumped up and went across the room to look at a vase of roses. A servant opened the door, stood back, announced:

"Mr Peter Carey."

"All alone?" said the old lady as he came over to shake hands with her. "Where is the faithful Hubert?"

"Faithful or fateful?" he asked, sitting down by her after he had shaken hands with Patricia. "He's portentously solemn the last few hours. By the way, I was to present his compliments and tell you that business detained him, much against his will."

"He is not forgiven!"

Patricia smiled across at him. "Mrs Elphinstone is in a terribly severe mood today, Mr Carey. She has just been giving me a lecture."

"You must be the last person to need one," he said.

"Absolutely, but the first to receive any that are hanging about in the offing."

"We hear sad news of you, Mr Carey," said Mrs Elphinstone. "A little bird has been flying about."

"Does he wear a tail-coat by day and take an interest in the law?" smiled Peter.

"Little birds wear no identification marks, Mr Carey. But is this a truthful bird? Is it true that you are on the point of perpetrating an elopement?"

Peter grinned. "Miss Repton, you must help me. You did it, you know."

"Hush!" cried Patricia. "I have just been telling Mrs Elphinstone that I had nothing whatever to do with it."

The old lady nodded. "And I believe her. From the biased account she gives of her doings, she merely found a lady who thinks she has a claim to something you have bought."

"I put it to you," said Peter lightly, "am I to allow even a business rival to waste her substance in riotous travelling, when she can have a share of my porters at a nominal rate? Put yourself in my place."

She laughed at him. "I have always refused to do anything of the kind. Persistent effort of that kind leads to penury, and who knows what else. A little altruism is a dangerous thing—and more is worse!"

Peter Carey thoughtfully rubbed one knee. "Where is Mr Elphinstone today?" he asked. "I should have an ally in him."

"That is why I sent him out to his club—though I am not sure you would. But come! he travels fastest who travels alone, and it seems to me unwise to burden your safari with a lady."

"Or contrariwise," said Peter, not at all put out. "You see, the lady knows Africa, and I don't, and we have Townard to guide us."

Patricia smiled at him. "I'm neutral. I have already told Mrs Elphinstone so. I even went further with your cousin, and suggested going out, too, to chaperon the party."

He looked at her quickly. "I suppose you shocked Hubert?"

"Immensely." Pat turned again to Mrs Elphinstone. "Can't you see that something has already happened? Mr Carey looks mildly ashamed of himself. I have a conviction that we are behind the fair this time."

"What's this, Mr Carey—is it a true bill?"

Peter grinned again. "I am afraid it is, rather. You see, Mrs Gores wrote me a letter. I got it this morning. She accepted my offer, and I answered at once."

"You have forgotten to post it!" cried the old lady hopefully.

"I am no mere man," he laughed. "When I write, I post."

"He was afraid Mr Gage-Chipnell might stop him," said Pat.

"There is something in that," said Peter, as tea came in. "I take the line of least resistance."

"Your chin doesn't say so!"

The old lady amused him. "I must wear a chin-strap at night, to make it less prominent," he said gravely. "It seems to give me away, a sin unforgivable in any chin. Think what a loser I should be at poker with such speaking features!"

Patricia dimpled. Peter was apparently less serious of mind than she had at first thought him. "I'll chance a future lecture and congratulate you," she said. "That poor soul really did intend to risk her little bit on a gamble. And I for one, don't believe you are going to elope."

"Traitor!" cried the old lady.

Peter bowed. "In return, let me promise you the first news, if I think of something of the kind."

A visitor came in as he spoke; an elderly lady dressed in late Edwardian style, who greeted Mrs Elphinstone with effusion. She had Patricia and Peter introduced to her, then sat close by her hostess, and launched out on an interminable account of a nephew. Patricia could not be sure if he were gracious or graceless, but he was evidently the apple of his aunt's eye, and, to judge by her looks, a *bete noir* of Mrs Elphinstone's. At any rate, she drew the fire from Peter, and he looked distinctly relieved when the nephew took the place of the widow in the conversation.

"I suppose I have tied myself up," Peter murmured to Pat as the Edwardian lady got up verbal steam.

"You have," Patricia agreed with a smile. "But I am sure Mrs Gores would let you off if you asked her nicely."

"I wasn't thinking of Mrs Gores," he said. "You are as suspicious as the others."

"What were you thinking of, then?"

"Myself principally."

She twinkled. "Said by some women to be man's one occupation."

He smiled. "I meant tied myself up to this jaunt, solus, or in company."

"Mrs Gores will be very disappointed. In any case, you were so keen to go. Aren't you now?"

Peter looked round at the two old ladies and bit his lip. "In a way, yes. Of course—yes. I'd fixed up to leave in a fortnight. It's horribly near."

"Near what?" asked Patricia innocently.

He did not pursue the subject. "Of course, I don't intend to stay there indefinitely. I don't see why I shouldn't be back in nine months, a year at most. If I am the owner, I must get back to look into the question of finance."

"Of course," said Patricia.

He looked away. "Interested in Africa at all?"

"I have never had much chance to be," she said.

"I meant would it interest you if I sent you a few notes; ah, about the scenery, and so on? It will be new to me. I thought of keeping a diary, or something like that."

"Rather jolly," she murmured.

Somehow she felt less afraid of Peter's "elopement." He gave her a smile now, and went on:

"You wouldn't mind if I sent them on; the bits I thought might interest you?"

"I should love it," she said. "Please do."

He stared at his boots. "I wondered if you would acknowledge them now and again. Not every packet, you know, but every couple of months."

"Oh, I won't be rude, if that is what you mean," she said.

Peter looked very young again. "Top-hole," he said. "Just a note, you know. Of course you may hear about my doings from Hubert, but I would rather like that too."

Patricia could have hugged him for his ingenuousness. "Occasionally I might even tell you of my doings," she dimpled.

"Better still," said Peter, laughing when he found that she was gently pulling his leg. "I'd really like to keep in touch."

Patricia nodded and changed the subject. "You won't like

telling your cousin about your decision, will you?"

He pursed his lips. "In a way, no. But of course, though Hubert has been jolly kind, I'm not his legal ward. I don't say he doesn't mean well. He does. But your man of the world is too cynical, Miss Repton. He pictures me to himself as a callow young thing, in constant danger of being married by *force majeure*. But really, I haven't met with many cave-women."

"The cave-woman is an invention of the disgruntled married man," said Patricia, much amused. "He tells the world that Eve did all the persuading. But Adam's a bit of a fruitarian himself if he would only admit it."

"At any rate, I'm booked for this trip," said Peter, replacing his tea-cup on the tray. "The sooner I start, the sooner I get back."

She laughed. "The pioneering spirit is waxing weak very early. But I must not tease you, in view of the Caudle lecture due from Mr Gage-Chipnell."

"Back me up!" said Peter.

"Do my best," she assented.

Mrs Elphinstone was dying to return to the attack, but the chance visitor was now launched on an account of her family and relations of all degrees, and at the end of an hour Peter got up to go.

The Edwardian lady did not, and Mrs Elphinstone made no comment of a detaining kind.

"Any afternoon about this time, you will find me in," she told him as he said goodbye, "but I suppose you are busy?"

"Shockingly," he said. "I never knew one wanted so many things for this job. The White Knight will be travelling light compared with me."

He held out his hand to Patricia, and spoke more softly. "May I come round to your office one morning? I think we ought to run through those papers again, in the light of what Mrs Gores told us."

"Do," said Patricia. "But let me know by telephone when you are coming."

The Edwardian lady went at last, and Mrs Elphinstone turned

on Patricia a face of humorous wrath. "My dear, what a nephew! He was as ubiquitous as King Charles's head with Mr Dick. I pushed her off on to collateral lines, but we always came back to the nephew. And while we were busy, Mr Carey escaped!"

Patricia smiled gently. "A strategist."

"What were you two whispering about?" demanded the old lady. "I have told you what we said, so be kind."

"We were not vulgarly whispering," Patricia protested. "I never whisper to young men unless I know them very well."

Mrs Elphinstone snorted. "I suppose he was telling you how charming Mrs Gores is."

"No, he was merely asking if he might send me some accounts of the scenery he saw," said Pat.

"The only scenery that woman will let him see will be the liquid pools of her eyes—if they are liquid! I hope they aren't!" cried Mrs Elphinstone.

CHAPTER 14
OUTWARD BOUND

Even Hubert gave up his attempt to dissuade Peter from taking Mrs Gores with him as the days passed. He began to see a good deal of Patricia again, his cousin being very busy with the last preparations for a start.

Though he was not such a great favourite with the old lady as Peter, he was always welcome at the Elphinstones', and often managed to make his visits coincide with those of Patricia to her old friends. Once he took her to Lord's, and she dined with him and danced once at the Savoy.

Peter allowed eight days to pass before he turned up at the office with his papers. It came out then that he had necessarily seen something of Mrs Gores, and had already fixed up their passages.

Between them they had decided on their course of procedure. Peter had put their decision on paper and deposited it with her solicitor. It was to the effect that he agreed to abide by the decision of the chief whose lands were involved. If the decision was in his favour, he was to pay Mrs Gores two thousand down for her husband's services as a surveyor of the area, with an *ex gratia* payment of one per cent on the profits when the mine was exploited. If he found that the concession had never belonged to the man Hanaper, Mrs Gores agreed to refund him the ten thousand pounds he had paid, out of any money she might obtain for her rights.

"So, you see, she wants to do the square thing," he told Patricia. "That was her own suggestion. I have cabled out to Townard telling him that Mrs Gores is coming with us."

Patricia saw Mrs Gores herself, and could not help feeling that Hubert's fears were not without justification. It was not that the widow looked more designing than before, but, certainly, hope revived, and prosperity in prospect, had done wonders for her. Already she looked younger, smarter, and now one could say that she was handsome without qualification.

She had, she told Patricia, had an excellent offer for her house, and would get a reasonable sum for her furniture.

"Of course, I am keeping all poor Tom's things," she said, and the shadow that flitted over her face as she said that did reassure Patricia, "but I had to have an outfit, so I did not think of storing anything but those."

Patricia glanced at her frock. "What a charming frock that is," she said.

Mrs Gores dimpled. "I am so pleased to hear you say so. It is such a relief to have a little money. I got quite Couéd when I was living without friends; every day I got dowdier and dowdier!"

"I'm sure you exaggerate awfully," said Patricia smiling, but added more seriously, "I wonder if you would like me to keep any of your little souvenirs for you? I know one sends that kind of thing to store only under protest. I haven't a great deal of spare space in my flat, but I should be glad to help."

Mrs Gores looked grateful. "Would you? Oh, how kind of you. There are some things of Tom's I can't keep, even if they were his. His rifle, for example. The people out there were kind. They sent back everything, I think—his rifle, his watch, and signet-ring, even a box of spare ammunition for the rifle. Then there are the little things I got from him before. I think they would all go into a little packing-case, and I should be awfully grateful if you would take that till I get home again."

"Perhaps Mr Carey could get someone to buy the rifle; they are costly things, I believe."

Mrs Gores shook her head. "Do you know, I have an idea. I

wonder if Mr Carey would let me give him the rifle? I wouldn't give it to anyone else, but he has been so generous and good."

"You might try," said Patricia doubtfully. "Is it a heavy one?"

Mrs Gores nodded. "He wouldn't go shooting buffalo without one. It's a .577. It would have stopped the buffalo, only for the misfire, for Tom was a clinking shot."

Patricia looked at her. "What dreadful bad luck."

"So terrible, my dear," whispered Mrs Gores, the tears again in her fine eyes. "Someone had wounded it the day before, and it was tying up in thick bush to one side of a game-path, they wrote me. Tom was looking for signs of it, and Lepper had his gun. The buffalo charged, and Lepper handed it to him. From the details I got, I think Tom had time to get in one shot. Then came the misfire. He hadn't another chance. . . ."

Patricia saw how moved she was, and began hastily. "It will be a pleasure to keep the things for you. Do let me. Just tell me when they will come, and I will arrange to have them kept if I am out."

Mrs Gores thanked her, and was brave again. Unless she was a consummate actress, she was indeed still in love with the mere memory of her husband. Hubert and Mrs Elphinstone were wrong. There was no danger.

"I hear Mr Carey is going out very soon now," she said.

Mrs Gores nodded. "What a mercy he has that man Townard to make preparations. We're going to Kilindini, you know— Mombasa. And then we shall use the Uganda railway part of the way, before we go into the blue."

"You are not at all nervous?"

"I? No, not at all. I am made like that. Besides, it is only when we really strike into the bush that there is any danger. If I were subject to fevers, I don't know how I should feel about it, but thank goodness, I'm not."

Patricia felt more reassured after that interview, but two little troubles took the place in her mind of the uncertainty created by Hubert's croakings and Mrs Elphinstone's fears. Why, in the first place, should she trouble about the matter at all? In the second place, was she going to lose her head over Peter Carey?

Falling in love with a man who is setting out on a very long trip within a few weeks of meeting you is a parlous business. The younger generation is not less romantic than the old. It only thinks it is. The world is still well lost for love, even in hearts that prefer slang to sentiment. The thing isn't done—but it happens.

Patricia would fall in love with a man who would set every purpose aside for her. At least, she thought so. She tried to compare Peter with Hubert, and couldn't. Hubert was assessable. He was what you saw, and that was very nice. But we weary of just what we can see. Peter, for all his naïveté, was not so easily to be weighed on the scales. His face slid into Patricia's memory again, that faint smile, the grey eyes with their attractive twinkle at times. But it was sheer nonsense to imagine him making love to Mrs Gores. He wasn't that kind.

Patricia had been excited by Inspector Hoes visit, but he did not turn up again until four days before the date fixed for Peter's departure, and then he came suddenly and without notifying her in advance.

Patricia had been talking to Miss Froud, telling her jokingly that the one stroke of business had finished their luck, when Hoe came in.

He wore a morning-coat, with a flower in the buttonhole, striped trousers, a silk hat. He looked like a large stockbroker, and had rather a presence thus dressed.

Patricia at once took him into her private office, and made him sit down.

"You've come to tell me something," she said.

He nodded. "I thought you would like to know how the Willesden inquiry is progressing, miss."

"Awfully," she agreed eagerly. "Is there anything in it, the other house business, I mean?"

He nodded again. "Absolutely, miss. There weren't any fingerprints, which shows that the man was wearing gloves, but they do know now someone got into the house and into that room in the return."

"Good. But no one saw him, I suppose?"

106

"No one seems to have done. That's our trouble. What we have to go on is only conjecture, and it may be quite out. You remember I told you I wondered if a confederate had killed this man Hanaper?"

"Of course I do."

"You will remember, too, when you called on me at the Yard, I told you one of our people recognised the dead man as a fellow who went under the name of Williams?"

"Yes, I do. You said he had a pal called Trevor, who stuck to him and refused to implicate him."

"So he did. If it hadn't been for Trevor's denial, and the lark of direct evidence against Williams, or Hanaper, there would have been two convictions instead of one."

"That was two years ago?"

"Round about. I have looked it up, and it was exactly two years and three months."

"And the man Trevor got eighteen months?"

"You have a good memory, miss. That makes his release date about nine months ago."

Patricia nodded. "Why do you bring him in?"

Hoe looked at her and smiled. "Don't you see, he may be a link? He may have been the man in the next return."

"Do you think so?" she said, starting. "But why should you fix on him?"

Hoe shrugged. "Well, miss, criminals have to choose their pals, or tools, with some care; and they don't change oftener than they can help. If one cuts up rough with the other, or double-crosses him, he can't swear the offended one won't tip us off and chance it."

"In there no honour among thieves?" she smiled.

"Precious little, miss, except in books. Sometimes they are pretty loyal to one another, but it is generally from motives of safety."

"But this man Trevor suffered alone for what you suspect they had both done."

"He did, but it wouldn't make his punishment any lighter to

have Hanaper in jail with him. Besides, when two professionals work together, they find it more profitable to have one out of clink."

"But I don't see why."

His eyes twinkled. "The one who is out can look round for new mugs while the other is in clink. When the prisoner is released he will find 'work' waiting for him."

"I see. But this man Trevor is, you think, the murderer?"

"I think he may be. You see, we have a double confirmation here. I told you a criminal might kill a pal who had double-crossed him; he would be still more likely to do it if he had stuck by him in the past and got him off a sentence."

"I see what you mean."

"Say," continued the Inspector, "Williams, alias Hanaper, and he prepared this swindle, and were to go fifty-fifty. Your pal hands over the money. Trevor comes along to collect his share. Williams refuses to part up; perhaps he is going to scoot. Trevor is furious, and decides to do him in, hoping perhaps, as I said, to take the whole swag."

"Well, why didn't he?"

Hoe shrugged. "If he didn't, it was largely because that terrace had been built by two different builders."

Patricia laughed out. "Why, you are as good as Sherlock Holmes."

"Oh, there is nothing clever about it, and it wasn't my doing, either. I mean that the house where Hanaper stayed had been the end one in the terrace at one time, and waste land beside it. When they began to build on, and continue the terrace, different people owned it, and the houses were planned a little different."

"But there was a return, with a kitchen and a bedroom over in both?"

"Quite right, miss. The builder put on a return in the new lot, partly for uniformity, and partly because it was convenient in view of the narrow plots. But he had a water-pipe leading down from the eaves gutter, and running past the window. The pipe in the house where Hanaper was ran down at the end of the return out of reach."

"So that he could climb into the window of one return, but not into that opposite?"

"That's it exactly. He couldn't afford to hang about much before the murder, in case someone should spot him and give evidence after. He must have had a glance at the house that was empty that night from the back, and he might assume that both had convenient water-pipes. But, when the shot was fired, he had no chance to do anything but revenge himself."

"I hadn't thought of that," said Patricia. She was much interested now. It had never occurred to her before that the crimes one read of in the papers had so many ramifications. One expected the police to arrest the criminal, but hardly appreciated the ingenuity, the patience and cleverness that built up the case preceding the arrest.

"Now, our point is this," he went on evenly. "We try to keep an eye on the fellows who come out, if they come to town. But Trevor doesn't seem to have tried his luck in London. He vanished into the country on his release, and has not been heard of since. Of course he may have had a bit put away, and gone down into the country. We can't expect the country police to keep tab on every crook."

"But he was bearded, wasn't he?"

He grinned. "He won't be now!"

"How silly of me! Of course not. I suppose these people can make up a bit?"

"A little is better than a lot. Too much make-up gives a crook away to us, but very small changes alter a face a good deal, and if he can keep his fingers off things he has a chance."

"If he was Hanaper's pal, do you think he could possibly be a man who was out with Mr Gores, the engineer, on the concession I told you about?"

He stared. "You didn't tell me about him."

Patricia told him briefly. He looked very thoughtful, but he shook his head. "Trevor was in prison then. There is no mistake about that. But Hanaper wasn't, and Hanaper came from Africa, though what that kind of shark would be doing up in the bush I have no idea."

"Then you think it was Hanaper?"

"Who else could it be? He had the documents, and Lepper was the only white man with Gores when he died, according to your story. It seems to me he was Hanaper, and he stole the things, and came on home to negotiate them. He may have known Gores was on the track of something good, and thrown himself in his way, so as to get attached to the caravan."

Patricia thought it very likely. "It's a pity we don't know what he was like. But I could ask Mrs Gores if you wish."

"If you would, miss, I should be very grateful," he said. "We don't want too many folk to know of this, because it is all in the air yet. But it is my opinion that Trevor got in touch again with Hanaper when he was released, and did what I said. If he had only been obliging enough to leave his fingerprints on something, we should have him. But we'll carry on. He has been in town. I'll swear, and now it's up to us to get out our nets and make a sweep."

"Down in the East End?" she asked.

"Not likely," he said. "Trevor would be as out of place there as a bat in Trinity House. No, miss, the confidence man has his own beats."

Patricia looked at him anxiously. "Doesn't this rather suggest that my friend Mr Carey has been sold a pup?"

He nodded. "A sparrow painted like a canary. I'm afraid he will lose his money chasing this wild-cat."

"Luckily he can spare it, and he has been anxious to go out to Africa, anyway," she remarked. "But he and Mrs Gores have fixed it up on a mutual basis, so that neither of them can lose all, if the concession itself is real."

"Good!" said he, rising. "I don't like a gentleman to lose his money when he is so nice about it. Anyway, Williams, alias Hanaper, is dead, and we have only Trevor to look for. Once we get on his track we should have him all right. If he has been in retirement in the country he may likely break back there, and settle down till the next coup is due."

Patricia nodded. "That part I can leave to you. I will ask Mrs Gores about Lepper at once, and ring you up. Can you tell me the number?"

He took a card from his pocket and handed it to her. "It's very good of you, miss. Be sure I'll let you know anything that develops if it isn't an official secret."

"That's all I ask," said Patricia, as she showed him out.

When he had gone she told Miss Froud she would be away for an hour or two, and went up to Hampstead.

Mrs Gores was in, packing, as it happened, the souvenirs of her husband which Patricia had offered to store.

"By the way," said the latter, after they had chatted for a few minutes, "you never told me what that man Lepper was like. I wonder was he Hanaper? You know I did before."

Mrs Gores looked thoughtfully at her. "I think I could find it in Tom's old letters, but I am sure he did not say much. If I remember rightly, he said when he found him he looked a 'frowsty beggar with a long ragged beard.' That was all. Tom wasn't great at description, unless it was something to do with his business. But, like you, I am sure now it was that ruffian who shot himself accidentally."

Patricia had to be content with that. Lepper at least had been bearded, though beards might not be the only wear in the wilds.

"Did you ask Mr Carey about the rifle?" she said, a minute before she left.

"Yes, I did. Fancy you remembering! He was awfully nice about it, but he wouldn't let me give it as a present. So, in the end, he said he would take ten pounds off my passage money—and then the gun was a gift. It was, really; for it cost Tom forty guineas four years ago, and was in splendid condition."

"Well, I am glad you settled it," said Patricia, rising. "By the way, I shall see you again before you go, I hope?"

Mrs Gores smiled. "A friend of Mr Carey's, really your friend, I believe, is having us all to dinner. I am to meet the famous Mr Hubert Mr Carey talks of so often."

"The Elphinstones," said Patricia. "Well, you will like them. They are dears."

But she told herself as she went out that Hubert had engineered the thing without doubt. He wanted to have a look at the widow who might run away with his beloved Peter!

CHAPTER 15 AN ONLOOKER

At that farewell dinner Mrs Gores sat on the right of her host. Hubert sat next to her; on the other side of the table were Patricia and Peter Carey.

Courtly old Mr Elphinstone was charmed with Mrs Gores. He, at least, did not think her designing or dangerous, and after the first fifteen minutes Mrs Elphinstone obviously agreed with him.

Mrs Gores wore a simple black evening frock. Her arms and shoulders were very white. She was attractive but simple, the old man said to himself, and liked her quiet voice and her attention to him. What Hubert thought is another matter, but Patricia at the other side of the table was pleased to see that her new friend had made a pleasant impression.

She herself had bought a frock for the occasion, and Peter's eyes showed that he knew and approved it. He talked very gaily to her; more rapidly and gaily than ever before. She could not say if the prospect of the adventures ahead excited him, but noticed that his cousin glanced over once or twice as if in mild surprise.

Later on, it was Mr Elphinstone who rose and proposed the health of the venturers, and success to their quest. He spoke in his old-fashioned way of Argosies to distant seas, made recondite references to Prester John and the Queen of Sheba, ending up with a reference to latter-day poverty and coppers succeeding to the reign of gold.

The fact that coppers were made of bronze did not trouble him. They laughed and clapped him, and Peter made the shortest speech on record, thanking him and the others.

Patricia laughed at him. "Mr Carey, bring some gold back for me."

He smiled back. "I don't want to go now."

"Duty first!" she said. "When you are aboard tomorrow you will feel as keen as ever. We're going on to the theatre now. Mr Elphinstone insisted."

"Good!" said Peter, who liked most things. "Mrs Gores seems to have made a hit with them," he added in a low voice, seeing that his hostess was talking with Hubert.

Patricia looked at Mr Elphinstone, who was talking to Mrs Gores. "Decidedly. I am glad. Isn't it funny that I can't wish you both luck?"

"Rather. It is odd! But I don't know. We've worked out our agreement so that neither of us loses much. So perhaps you can wish me luck, and a safe journey back."

"Then I do," said Patricia. "Only you mustn't take such very long views. Think that you may be a millionaire."

"There are other roles I could fill with more pleasure," he said. "But don't let us worry any more about the old journey. I've had so much to do in advance I have got rather fed up with it already."

There was a general rising then, and ten minutes later they were on their way to the theatre.

In the Elphinstones' box, of course, Hubert's strategy went for nothing. Mrs Elphinstone put Patricia and Peter together, Mrs Gores sat with Hubert. Patricia was surprised rather than dismayed when she found herself approving this move. She felt pleased to be beside Peter. She was amazed to discover that the thought of his going depressed her. When she glanced at him she did not wonder so much. He was oddly attractive physically, and his liking for her was obvious enough to breed reciprocity. She liked the boy in him, and the man. It was that combination of strength and ingenuousness that had at first attracted her.

"I am sorry you are going, of course," she said softly, and then felt that she had said it too sincerely. It ought to have come in a lighter tone, not so much from the heart.

He looked at her gratefully. "Somehow, I like to hear you say that as if you meant it."

"I do, naturally," she achieved more flippancy now with an effort. "You are my first client."

"Is that all?" said Peter. "Aren't you going back on that very nice remark?"

"Of course there are other reasons," she said, feeling that Hubert's eyes were fixed on her. "But they are all nice reasons, and then, it isn't as if you were going away for a lifetime."

Peter smiled. "You promised to write, didn't you?"

"Did I?" she asked. "I thought I had only promised to acknowledge the bits of the diary you were going to send me; and only every two months or so?"

"With occasional accounts of your own doings," he reminded her. "I have a horribly accurate memory."

The orchestra stopped playing as he spoke, and the curtain rolled up. They had come in during the interval between the first and second acts.

During the greater part of the second act they were disentangling the motives of the characters which had been explained in the first. Mr Elphinstone and his wife hated the discourtesy of talking through a play, and the others became more interested in the doings on the stage as the play proceeded.

When the last interval came, Patricia looked down into the stalls. A levelled opera-glass caught her eye. It was directed at the box, she thought at first directed at her. Now she saw that someone below was staring at Hubert and Mrs Gores.

It was a lady in the back row. The upheld glass hid most of her face from Patricia, but she could see plump white arms and sweet shoulders, a mass of fluffy hair. The opera-glasses were not removed for a minute. Hubert was taking Mrs Gores into the foyer for a cigarette. He was standing up, putting her evening cloak about her shoulders. As he turned to the back of the box and went out, Patricia saw the glasses go down.

An idle curiosity turned to surprise as Patricia looked. The lady was about twenty-seven, handsome in a florid way. Her eyes struck Patricia most. They were big, they sparkled intensely, and even at this distance one would have said that they were furious.

Patricia wondered if that idea was exaggerated. But no. The emotions which had moved the looker-on did not die at once on her face. She was obviously alone, and under no necessity to restrain her feelings. Patricia did not know exactly what she saw in that face, except that it was a mirror for unpleasant reflections at that moment.

The woman looked away then, and she pointed her out to her companion.

"Do you see the woman in the back row of the stalls, Mr Carey? The fifth from this end."

He looked over. "Person in black and silver, do you mean, or the one in the rose?"

"Miss Black and Silver," said Patricia. "Do you know her? Have you ever seen her before?"

"No," said Peter, smiling. "Don't say she is sorry, too, that I am going, and having a last look at me?"

"Perhaps she knows Mrs Gores," said Patricia. "She had a jolly good stare up here."

Mr Elphinstone leaned forward to speak. "What do you think of the play, Patricia?"

"Oh, charming," she assured him. "I like it ever so."

Mrs Elphinstone patted her shoulder. "So glad, my dear. But now, for this act, I want you to talk to Mr Gage-Chipnell. Do you mind?"

"Not a bit," said Patricia. "Mr Carey, I am moving on."

"I want to talk to Mr Carey," said the old lady, "and my husband is anxious to hear the ending of something Mrs Gores was telling him at dinner just as I got up."

Hubert came back with his companion at that moment; the members of the orchestra were already in their seats. As the exchange of seats went on in the box, Patricia glanced down at the woman in the back stalls and again met the focussed glasses. But they were on her this time. Hubert did not glance down. He set himself at once to entertain Patricia, and seemed in surprisingly good spirits considering that he had, up to the last, objected to the joint expedition that set off on the morrow.

"Have you changed your mind?" said Patricia softly.

"Quite," said Hubert gaily. "I have taken off all the danger signals, and the line is clear."

"I'm glad," she said. "I knew you would come round to my point of view."

"I hope I shall always come round to that," he murmured.

"Don't be too sure," she rallied him. "I'm not."

"Even a difference with you might be charming," he said, his eyes merry.

"Don't be too sure of that, either," she replied. "I have a ferocious way with people who don't agree with me."

As the third act began and went on its way, Patricia felt sure that she and Hubert were again the objects of scrutiny. In the half-dark of the stalls below she saw a duplicate flash of the stage-lightning on the lenses in the last row.

She felt sure that the lady in silver-and-black knew Hubert, and was jealous of him. She might have cause, she might not, for jealousy is often the most unreasonable thing in the world. It was not her affair, in any case, though it was some time before she forgot the impression made on her by the sight of those wide, glaring eyes.

Then the curtain fell, the lights went up, the curtain rose again on the principal players waiting to take their calls. Patricia looked down. The lady in the stalls had gone, her seat gaped empty. She turned to find Hubert holding up her cloak.

"I'm taking Peter home," he said. "If you have tears, prepare to shed 'em now, Miss Repton!"

"Unfeeling brute!" said Peter, coming forward. "I'm going to take Miss Repton down to the car."

He went out of the box with her quietly. "Well, it seems funny to think this will be our last meeting for at least nine months," he said, as they went down the stairs. "But I'm jolly well going to hurry back, you know."

"Don't forget to write up your diary," she said, laughing, but feeling strangely sorry too. "'No day without a line,' as someone has said. I am looking forward to enjoying the scenery by proxy."

"The scenery?" he said vaguely. "Oh, I forgot. Of course. I say, what luck that I didn't meet you before."

"Is that a compliment?" she smiled.

"I mean what rotten luck," he said. "Just like me to put it back to front. But here's the Elphinstones' car. I remember the number."

He began to talk ten to the dozen. The Elphinstones came up. Hubert was also giving Mrs Gores a lift in his car. Mrs Elphinstone was always fussy about keeping anyone or anything waiting, and she touched Patricia on the shoulder. She and her husband had already said goodbye to Mrs Gores, and wished her luck in the enterprise.

"The car, my dear!"

She shook hands with Peter, and so did her husband. Patricia had a confused recollection after of a very strong grip, of Peter's rather set face looking into hers, of a murmur she could not quite catch.

She felt that she had been absurdly emotional in the last minute, and hoped Peter hadn't noticed it. Afterwards, too, she wondered if she had forgotten to say goodbye to Mrs Gores. Actually, she had done her duty properly but vaguely. She had never been like that before. She had prided herself on her poise. But, of course, it might only be the result of the excitement, the fuss about the car that had attended the leave-takings.

Mercifully Mrs Elphinstone did not chaff her about Peter as they drove home. She was listening to her husband telling her about Tom Gores's death in the bush.

"I have always understood," he was saying in his precise voice, "that the African buffalo was extremely ferocious, even more so than the animal we have mistakenly called the King of Beasts. It shows, does it not, on what small issues our life turns? Mr Gores had killed dozens of beasts safely, then a misfire condemns him

118

to a ghastly death."

His wife shivered a little. "A terrible death, my dear."

"And she is so plucky," went on the old man, "she is taking up life again with a brave heart. I am indeed glad to know that Mr Carey has volunteered to help her."

Patricia nodded. "You see how right I always am."

Mrs Elphinstone pinched her arm gently. "We can't say that till we hear more," she said. "Is Mr Carey going to write to you as he promised?"

"My dear!" cried Mr Elphinstone in gentle distress.

CHAPTER 16 HOE WONDERS WHO

On the very day that Peter Carey and his companion sailed for East Africa, some business came into Patricia's office, to startle the latter and afford Miss Froud much gratification.

"For, you know, Miss Repton," protested the conscientious one, "I am doing nothing here, and I am not earning what you give me."

Patricia had smiled. "No, but I am not paying you to do work that isn't here. I pay you for your time."

All the same, Miss Froud was pleased when a gentleman came in, and had an hour's interview with her employer.

Fortunately for this caller he told Patricia at once that he had heard of her from a friend of the Elphinstones. Otherwise Patricia would have surveyed his proposition through a powerful microscope, almost have submitted it to a financial bacteriologist to make sure that it contained no germs of a swindle.

It was not a very big thing, but it was marketable, and it kept Patricia busy for a little, and took her mind from other things. There was nothing speculative about it, and she soon found touch with a sound financier, who promised to go into it. This was a tonic to her pride, which had fallen so heavily over the Hanaper affair.

She was congratulated by her client on her grip of essentials, while the financier did not attempt to make love to her, or leer at her after the fashion of some former callers. All this kept off the threatened attack of cold feet, and determined her to stick to her job until she had proved herself competent.

She had rather expected to be rung up by Hubert Gage-Chipnell that week, but business or something kept him away, and she saw nothing of him for nine days. He had gone down to see his cousin off, but she saw no more of him just then.

Patricia had neither illusions nor delusions. She knew that Hubert admired her. He had made that plain enough. She was rather pleased that he did not make the running too much now, for her emotions were still in a fluid state, and she found herself thinking much oftener of Peter Carey.

Even when she went to the Elphinstones' Hubert did not turn up, as he had had a habit of doing before. They had not seen him either, though he had written a little note to Mrs Elphinstone telling her that a serious case was absorbing his attention.

Mrs Gores's souvenirs turned up at Patricia's flat the day the travellers sailed. When she came back from her office that evening a small packing-case stood in the flat.

Mrs Gores had left her quite free to store the things *en bloc* or dispose them about her rooms. Patricia took the latter course with some of the smaller and more delicate things. The case had not been well packed, and rough handling on the way had resulted in a broken lid and a nasty crack in the side.

Patricia promptly wrote a letter of protest to the forwarding agents, and took out the contents of the case with some trepidation.

Two jars of native pottery on top were smashed, but might be mended. The glasses of two or three photographs were cracked across. Those also could go to a shop to be repaired. Charging herself with that job, she set them aside.

When all were out she surveyed the pile on the floor, and began to sort the heavier and stronger articles from the more delicate and fragile. The former would go back into the case, and remain in a cupboard. The other things she would keep out.

Half an hour found the pile mostly removed from the floor.

She hesitated a moment with a last small package, a box of rifle ammunition which had been opened and tied up again.

She read the bore on the label, ".577," and shrugged. "I don't suppose she meant to keep this. It is no good to her. I wonder she didn't give it to Mr Carey with the rifle," she said to herself.

It was a morbid souvenir at the best, and she did not think Tom Gores's widow was morbid. Half a dozen cartridges from the box had been used. She was not sure if these things in their heavy brass cases would be dangerous in case of fire. She knew enough about sport to know that they would not go off of themselves.

She shrugged, put the box into the three-quarter-filled case, and consulted the list of items Mrs Gores had given her. She checked it, laid some paper parcels containing native grass-work on top of the box, and put the lid on the case once more. Then she managed to drag it to a cupboard, pushed it back as far as it would go, and began to arrange the other souvenirs in her bedroom.

The next day she was going to a dance with Dick Caley, the young fellow in the Foreign Office. She meant to ask him again about the rumour of tse-tse at Bangele. Hanaper had laughed at it, but the dead Hanaper was now suspect. It would not do to take his word for granted.

"You may be right, old thing," said Dick next evening, as they drove away together, "but I see you are still perpetuating a villainous error in mistaking the FO for that other haunt known as the Colonial Office. We deal with the affairs of great nations; nothing smaller. Last time you phoned over I had to communicate with a colleague in the other show."

Patricia laughed. "Don't let FO stand for Fat Occiput, or swelled head," she warned him. "But could I make sure by inquiring at what you call the other show?"

Dick grinned. "Probably not. Ours is the abode of efficiency. The CO we know nothing about. If you are really keen on knowing if the tse-tse still barges round Bangele, you might go and see one of the highbrows at the Institute of Tropic

Medicine."

"I will," said Patricia. "Thanks for the tip. I ought to have thought of it myself."

"Like me, you have your occasional lapses," said Dick Caley. "By the way, I saw you at the theatre the other night, mixing your drinks. First you sat next a merchant who looked too good to be true, and then another who looked good but not true."

"I went with the Elphinstones. Why didn't you come round to see us?"

"I was busy. You seemed busy too, or you might have seen me. I was in the stalls at the far side, and I waved a programme twice, and only got the cold eye for my trouble.—Oh, Nelson, you broke my heart!"

Patricia laughed. "You are all brains and no heart at the FO I understood."

"Well, this is where we gambol," said he, as the taxi-cab stopped. "Let the great brain translate itself into mazy steps!"

Next day Patricia did go to the Institute as he had suggested, and interviewed a bald young man, who was only physically highbrow, and very obliging.

"Your informant is right," he said, when he had looked up some data, "Here our statistics are kept up to date. Naturally government offices concentrate on administration rather than sanitation."

"Then Bangele is clear of fly?"

"So far as we know, yes. There was a serious outbreak in 1903, but, for some reason or other, we have not heard of any recurrence. I have an idea that a good deal of the bush was cut down. At all events we have no knowledge of any present danger. I think you said your informant had been out lately?"

"Not so long ago. He joined a safari."

"Anyone of experience at the head of it?"

"Oh yes, a well-known mining engineer, who surveyed a concession there."

The young man nodded. "That gives you the answer in itself. You could neither get nor keep native labour in fly-country, and no one would willingly take a safari through it, let alone think of exploiting it. You are aware, of course, that heavy work is not done in Africa by white labour, and the administration would prevent any recruiting for an area that was suffering from sleeping-sickness."

He had really been very kind and informative, and Patricia thanked him warmly as she went away. She felt happier now about Peter Carey and his companion. The logic of the man at the ITM was unassailable.

Dick Caley had led her astray in the first instance, but then she had made a mistake in applying to him, when the facts lay ready to her hand in the useful ITM.

She went back to her office, to find the managing clerk of a law firm awaiting her. He had called about the new business she was offering, and was presently deep with her in legal points.

It was lunch time when she presently got him away. She took an hour, and came back to find Miss Froud talking to the redoubtable Inspector Hoe.

Once or twice in the past week she had asked herself why Hoe had attached himself to her to this extent. She had an idea that he was deep and clever, behind his large and bland exterior. Then why did he think it necessary to keep her so constantly in touch with details that most concerned his own department? There was no answer to that at the moment.

Miss Froud immediately went out for her own lunch, and Patricia showed Hoe into her office and closed the door.

"You are certainly keeping your word," she smiled, as he sat down, "aren't you?"

"I try to, miss," he said, "and I thought you might like to know that our country fishing has resulted in a mild bite—just a nibble."

"About the man Trevor?"

"Yes, miss. We had to start at the jail, but a bit of luck threw us in with a man who had seen Trevor on the road. He was a tramp, this fellow, and fell into talk with the released prisoner. He left him at Partley Station, where Trevor went in."

"That's about twenty miles out of Holdleham?" she said.

"Yes. We made a list of the stations going both ways on that line, and then we made enquiries at each."

"Any luck?"

"Yes. At a small station in Wiltshire, Ceorpham by name, we heard that a man answering to his description had got out."

Patricia shook her head. "But surely—so long ago?"

He smiled. "That's what we thought at first, miss. But the man had gone to a little cottage on the Downs five miles off, and was seen now and again at the station, where his was sent."

"Did he buy the cottage?"

"No, but someone else did, and from his description I should say it was Hanaper. He bought it in the name of Jasper, the name Trevor took down there."

"But what about money?"

"Ah, there I don't know, I think it is pretty likely that Trevor had got his pal to leave some of his money hidden in the cottage. The place was bought a month before his release, and locked up till he came to it."

"Splendid!" she cried warmly, "Is he there now?"

He shook his head. "I said we had had a nibble. Trevor left the cottage three months ago, letting it to a lady who wanted to paint."

"Can you trace him further?"

He shrugged. "Well, we have got a good start, bridging those six months. The later a man is seen, the easier he is to trace, and we have all the country police notified."

"What is he like?" she asked.

He pulled a photograph from his pocket. "He may be a good deal different from this, but it isn't bad of him as he was. You will see he is clean-shaven. Take a good look at him. I don't say it will do any good, but people living in town do see a wonderful assortment of people."

"Besides, as you said, he has to carry on his nasty profession where moneyed people are," she said, as she studied the photograph.

"Yes, and if he thinks we are not looking for him, he might turn up in restaurants and places where they dine in the West-End."

She handed back the photograph. "I think I might know him if I saw him."

"I don't suppose you will," said he, replacing it in his pocket. "But I have been worrying over someone else since I saw you last, miss."

She looked at him interestedly. "Who is that?"

"Our dead friend Hanaper and the other dead man, Mr Gores."

Yes, he was deep. There was something subtle about this large policeman with the brooding grey eyes. Patricia had a sudden feeling that there was more iron than fat in his composition.

"Why Mr Gores?" she asked softly.

He nodded once or twice, and began to run his large fingers over the edge of her desk.

"Well, you see, miss, it's too accidental as it stands. I don't say Mr Gores mightn't have picked up a lost European in the bush. It's happened a good many times, and will again. The trouble is that he picked up a man who called himself Lepper, that Lepper looks to us rather like Mr Hanaper; that Mr Hanaper turns up in town carrying documents about a concession that Mr Gores surveyed."

She nodded. "I know. We agreed last time, I think, that Hanaper might have followed up Gores so as to get with the safari."

"Very well. But if that is true, why should he do it? Because he knew Gores was on the trail of something good. That again suggests Gores' expedition was known of before he started. In fact, it must have been. What is the inference from that?"

"If Lepper was really Hanaper, that he intended to get the documents."

"Quite, but there were no documents then. Granted, however, that he meant to steal something valuable from Gores, he would know that he could not at any rate sell a concession belonging to Gores while the latter was still alive."

"But Gores was dead when he stole them; if he did."

"Right again, only we must go further than that, miss. Mr Gores was killed by a wounded buffalo charging him. Hanaper may have been clever, but he couldn't provide a convenient buffalo. If he was magician enough to do that, he could not say whether the animal would charge him or the other fellow."

"Where does that lead us? I confess that I don't see any answer."

"What I want to know is this," said Hoe decidedly: "Was Mr Gores killed by a buffalo at all?"

She started. "So Mrs Gores said. Her husband fired, at least tried to, but the gun misfired, and the buffalo got him."

Hoe looked sceptical. "I don't know exactly the nature of the wounds made by a buffalo, but I don't doubt they could be imitated by violence on the body of a dead man."

"You mean that he may have been killed by Hanaper?"

"I don't see why not. Hanaper must have known he had to get Gores out of the way before he could sell anything."

"What a ruffian!"

"If our theory is true," said Hoe, kindly including her with himself in the ownership of the theory. "Now, here is rather an important point. Did you gather that there were any other white men about when Gores was killed? I don't mean Lepper."

Patricia reflected for a moment. "No, I don't think so. Mr Pulter, an African official, had been killed falling into an elephant-pit. The letter did not speak of any other man—white man, that is."

CHAPTER 17 A SIN
OF COMMISSION

Inspector Hoe raised heavy eyebrows, though not in surprise. "Good, miss! So we have poor Mr Gores dead, and Lepper, or Hanaper, the only white man with him. Probably there were headmen and gun-bearers, beside the porters, but those would be natives of one kind or another."

"Obviously."

"Then who sent back his gold watch, and the other things; not to speak of his rifle?"

Patricia frowned. "Mrs Gores said 'they sent them back', but you know how loosely people use the plural when they are not very sure of the sender. I should have thought the natives would have kept the rifle and ammunition—they could have said their master lost them in the bush after the buffalo had charged?"

"Quite so. You mention ammunition?"

She told him of the broken box of shells for the heavy rifle. "It struck me as funny," she added.

He considered the point. "Yes. Odd! But there may have been a purpose in that. His sending the rifle and cartridges back may have been intended to stress in the widow's mind the idea that her husband was out with this very rifle, and was killed owing to a defective cartridge."

"But why should Hanaper take such precautions if he was out there? No one would trace him."

Hoe did not agree. "Porters, I know, may be got anyhow, but I have heard that the headmen and gun-bearers often engage time after time with other Europeans. Someone out from here might enquire about Tom Gores, and the headman describe Hanaper. By the way, I have cabled to Cape Town and Johannesburg to the police, telling them when Hanaper first came over, and asking them to trace his earlier career if they can."

"Would you like to see this ammunition?" asked Patricia.

"It can do no harm, miss, though I don't know that it will do any good."

Patricia nodded. "Will you come to my flat? I have the box there. If there is any possibility of Mr Gores having been murdered, I do think it is worth looking into."

They took a taxi to her flat, and she produced the box of ammunition. Hoe looked at it for a little, then asked if he might have it for a day or two.

"I can take it to the gunsmiths who sold it," he said. "They will perhaps give us an idea if any of it is defective. I know some powders deteriorate in a hot and damp climate. If the expert decides that the stuff is in good condition, it will be support for my theory."

"I don't know why Mrs Gores kept them, but she might not like them to be fired away," said Patricia.

"Oh, they have machines to unload them. They may fire one or two, but they can replace them with shells of the same kind. If the lady doesn't know, she won't grieve."

"Let me have them back again then as soon as you can. I don't know really if Mrs Gores thought of them all. It may be that she did not know what to do with them, or meant to give them with the rifle to Mr Carey."

"Oh, he has that, has he?"

"Didn't I tell you? But it must be all right, for Mr Carey is a shooting man, and familiar with firearms."

Hoe tied up the box more securely. "From your account of it, we may be sure Hanaper and Mr Gores were alone at the time. Even on the account given by letter to Mrs Gores, Hanaper was carrying the heavy rifle for Gores. If the natives were up that was the gun-bearer's job."

"I think they were alone. Perhaps Mr Gores had a light rifle, with the other in reserve."

"Then he would be in front, and this was spoken of as a game-path. What was to prevent Hanaper (behind in a narrow track) from clubbing the other fellow and making a mess of him? By that time the survey had been made and the papers completed. It was a temptation to a scoundrel like Hanaper."

Patricia nodded. "Oh, I think he was quite capable of it. He made a fool of me and I never suspected the kind of man he was. I could not understand at first why he should have failed to place such an excellent proposition in the City, and I actually thought at one time it might be fly-country, and that the reason why no one in the know would take it up."

Inspector Hoe smiled faintly. "'Fly' is a slang term for tricky or artful," he said. "So Hanaper led you into fly-country, even if there wasn't a tse-tse in it."

She laughed. "So he did. I quite agree with you. By the way, what will happen to the money the police found in Hanaper's room if Mrs Gores proves her case?"

Hoe reflected. "Then I don't see why she shouldn't claim it. It will be a little trouble, but, if she is the concessionaire, she was the vendor of the thing, and not the man who stole her title."

"Equally, Mr Carey will be the new owner?"

"That is so. If she claims and gets the money the consideration she gave for it is the concession. I don't know much about such things, but that is common sense."

Patricia assented. "What I cannot place is the man Trevor's share in this, if any. When Hanaper was acquitted under the alias Williams he must have left the country. Perhaps he went to Mombasa, as Mr Carey has done now. But he could not know at that time that Mr Gores had something very good in view. Besides, how did he know that I could get anyone to buy the thing?"

"He gave you the report of an expert," said Hoe. "If it is anything like the truth, the vendor would have been able to put down more than ten thousand."

"But there were contingent mine royalties when the thing became a paying proportion."

"Eyewash, miss. He wanted a lump sum, and then he would have cleared off. Being what he was, he may have made many enquiries about the lady who was starting for herself in the City, heard you had wealthy friends like Mr and Mrs Elphinstone, and determined to string you."

"He may have thought I would put them on to it?"

"Very likely. A lot of men don't give women any credit for brains. Probably he went to Trevor for help, and had to promise a share. We know what happened after that."

"And I can't be sorry now. All I fear is that the concession may have lapsed on Mr Gores' death."

"That isn't impossible. Some contracts are like that. Again, they are beginning to wake up there, a colleague tells me, to the difficulties that may lie in alienating land belonging to natives. The chief is the head, but he doesn't hold land as a landowner does here. His people live on it, and may object to it being sold over their heads."

"I see what you mean," she said. "But Mr Pulter, the local official, seems to have been there."

Hoe nodded. "I don't know much about it, as I said, but the colleague I spoke of was out once. He says the local commissioners and officers get a great many contradictory instructions. The administration is in a state of flux, and will be till the big-wigs decide finally to introduce a fixed code of land laws. It's a question of balancing between native rights and the necessary development of the country."

Patricia found him unexpectedly intelligent. She had thought before of detectives, even the higher officers, as merely sublimated policemen.

"Well, Mr Carey can bear it at the worst," she said. "Mrs Gores, of course, is not well off. So I hope she will find it all right after all."

He went away then, and it was three days before the box came back by registered post with a note enclosed.

In the note he told her briefly that the shells had been found in perfect condition, but added that the fact that six were gone made the test an imperfect one. "One misfire, I am informed, may happen in a batch of shells otherwise good." Those were his words; no doubt a repetition of what the gunmaker had told him. He said nothing about Trevor or any further investigations.

Patricia was busy again with the affair she was negotiating. At the end of the week she went to see Mrs Elphinstone, and found the old lady alone.

"Pat," said her old friend, "you are not at all the Circe I thought you were! You have let one of the enchanted escape!"

Patricia smiled, "Have I? Do you mean Mr Gage-Chipnell?"

"I do, my dear. We were both afraid he was going to cut out our favourite Peter Carey, and now we never even see him."

Patricia shrugged. "A shock to my vanity. But I expect I shall survive it," she replied lightly. "Perhaps I gave him too little encouragement!"

Mrs Elphinstone looked amused. "Let us give it a nicer name —altruism. Mr Gage-Chipnell saw that Mr Carey was in earnest, and gave way to him.—Does that sound like him?"

"Not at all," said Patricia.

"Or he has fallen in love with Mrs Gores. You must have noticed that he suddenly gave up his objections to the joint expedition!"

"But that would make him jealous, not complaisant. Try again!"

"Then he thought that you were in love with Mr Carey, and nobly passed out of your life, as they do in novels. He heard that you were going to exchange letters, murmured 'Bless you, my children! I am only concerned for your happiness', and retired to mourn."

"You are so imaginative!" protested Patricia. "The fact is probably that he had a busy time with cases at his office, and had to attend to them."

Whatever the reason, she saw nothing of Hubert Gage-

Chipnell for another fortnight. By that time she had had a cable from Peter Carey, telling her that they had reached Mombasa safely, found Townard unexpectedly forward, and were soon starting up-country.

She told Hubert that, when she met him one day in Bond Street. He smiled and raised his eyebrows.

"Really? I hadn't heard. At all events, it's good news. I thought they might be hung up at the coast for donkeys-years. But Peter was always a lucky man. My uncle fed out of his hand, while he could never stomach my legal tastes."

Patricia smiled. "I haven't seen you at the Elphinstones' lately. Don't you go there now?"

"Awfully busy," he said. "The stuff comes in thick and fast, and my two partners have chosen this rotten time to be ill.—If you see them, please tell them I hope to look them up one day soon."

He talked for a little, then went on his way. Patricia looked after him. He looked as bright and cheerful as before, but there was a difference somewhere. She could not have said exactly what it was, but she was conscious of it. As a suitor, if he had ever seriously thought of being one, he had fallen out. Or was he simply one of those men who indulge in furious flirtations and then hastily retire from the field?

Of course it did not matter to her. She liked him, but she knew now quite definitely that there had never been the shadow of a possibility of falling in love with him. She thought it would be difficult for any normal girl to dislike Hubert, who had a ready tongue, a flattering way when he wished, and a fund of good spirits.

Though she had smiled at Mrs Elphinstone's suggestion, it was just possible that Hubert had retired from the field when he saw that his cousin was in earnest. He was fond of Peter. And Patricia would have been blind if she had not seen that Peter had fallen in love with her.

Then a thought struck her, faintly amusing, and very possibly true. That girl in the stalls at the theatre had not been interested in her or Peter. She had been focussing her opera glasses on

133

Hubert and Mrs Gores first, and during the third act, when Patricia herself had sat with Hubert, she had stared at them.

Of course that was very likely. No doubt Hubert was an adept at flirting, had made mild love to many women. This one had taken it more seriously. She was jealous, and she had looked it. For all she knew, Hubert might be quietly engaged to the girl. The fact that he had not turned up at the Elphinstones' since, or sought her out, suggested that a fiancée in the background had read Hubert a little lecture on the virtues of constancy.

Patricia smiled again as she went to talk to Miss Froud. It amused her to think that Hubert might have a restraining apron-string attached to his volatile person.

"What am I to do now, Miss Repton?" the typist asked.

"You haven't learned the art of graceful idling," said Patricia. "I expect you are bored. Let me see.—Oh, yes. You might buy a book on concessions, a legal one, and modern. Then you can look through it, and make me copies of any passages that bear on our business. That will keep you busy until another client turns up, or we go bankrupt."

She went in to her own office and sat down. Her mind went back to the pertinacious Hoe. Was there anything in his theory that the death of Tom Gores could be laid at Hanaper's door?

The man might not have lacked the will, or been hampered by scruples.

She could think of no one of her acquaintance in London who had had experience with African big-game. Dick Caley and others had stalked in the Highlands, but that was no good at all. She thought suddenly of the Belgian, Eduard de Villegaile.

He was conversant with Africa. Could she count again on his chivalry and politeness if she asked him to help her with advice? It was worth trying, so she took up her desk-telephone, and rang up the offices of his company.

A clerk took her message, and told her to hold the line. She had repeated her name very clearly, and mentioned a former visit. M de Villegaile happened to be in a pleasant mood. He expressed himself willing to see her if she came round at once. He was desolated to say that in half an hour he had a meeting to attend, but he could give her twenty minutes. Patricia thanked him, and went round. She found him smiling and amiable.

"Mademoiselle honours me a great deal," he said, and she was not sure if his tone was not a trifle ironical.

"Worries you a great deal, you mean, monsieur," she said, smiling at him. "But those who are uniformly kind and polite lay themselves open to demands."

He laughed a little, and his bright eyes twinkled. "Mademoiselle is still interested in the continent that, for some national reason, her compatriots call Dark?" he said.

"I came to you because there are few men who know so much about it."

"You flatter me, mademoiselle."

"On the contrary. I pay you your due. You may remember that I spoke of Bangele, and the late Mr Gores, who surveyed an area there."

"Absolument. I myself have in the past had the pleasure of meeting Mr Gores."

"Well, you know he was killed by a wounded buffalo."

"But yes. You know the French proverb about the 'mechant animal'—or rather, the saying. Monsieur the Buffalo goes further on occasion—he attacks as well as defends, and sometimes without being attacked. Mr Gores was apparently foolish. He followed up the beast without having his rifle in his hand."

"Another man had it."

"Possible. That is all right in the plains, or in the open where one has space. One has a native in reserve with one's rifle, one falls back upon him, and arms oneself. But in a game-path, which may be no more than two feet wide, with bush to this side and that.—Has mademoiselle ever shot rabbits here?"

Patricia nodded. "Lots."

"Very well. Imagine a rabbit crossing a narrow ride in the bois —the wood. Flick! He is across! One shoots on the instant, or the lapin vanishes. The buffalo is not going to vanish. He emerges as fast as a rabbit, *at you*."

"That is the sort of thing I wanted to know," she said, eagerly. "I imagined that you might have had some experience."

He nodded. "I have shot seven buffalo, yes. And I think I have explained how this happened."

She nodded. "But I want some more information. Mr Gores did pull the trigger, but there was a misfire. How would that happen with a heavy rifle?"

"Powder that had deteriorated, perhaps."

"No, it wasn't that."

He smiled. "Then there is the detonator, the cap, a source of trouble often. If the combustible substance with which the cap is charged to detonate the powder is bad, there is a misfire."

"Who puts in these caps?"

"The maker, mademoiselle. He has machines for the whole process. On the other hand, if the action of the rifle was clog, or had gone wrong, possible that the blow of the plunger did not be sufficiently strong. Those are all the reasons that I know."

He looked up at the clock. Patricia rose, "I have lately made the acquaintance of Mrs Gores, the widow," she said. "So that is why I am anxious to know."

"Ah, the poor woman!" he murmured. "I can imagine her distress."

Patricia thanked him and went away. It struck her that she had taken up some of the poor man's time to no purpose. Rifles are fallible, and chemical products may deteriorate. It seemed probable that Hoe was right after all.

CHAPTER 18 A REFLECTION

Miss Froud had typed about a quarter of a fat volume of very legal aspect before any more business came into the office.

When it did come, it was in the nature of two or three very tired propositions, on their last legs with fatigue, contracted by being dragged from one financier to another. But Patricia accepted their sponsorship on the ground that it was good practice, and saved her from racking her brains for new work for Miss Froud.

She began at once to see if she could find someone willing to promote a company for the manufacture and exploitation of a gadget to keep the interiors of gas cooking-stoves free from grease.

But her thoughts were far from gas stoves and grease; with Inspector Hoe, who had not come again, with Peter Carey, who must now be on his way up-country. Her interest in heavy rifle ammunition had died a natural death. Tom Gores was dead, and Hanaper was dead. There was nothing to be done there.

At times, finding time hang heavy on her hands, she left her City office and went to the West-End. On one occasion, she enjoyed a shopping expedition with Mrs Elphinstone, and, in Harrods, caught a glimpse of the lady who had surveyed the occupants of their box so severely on the night of the last theatre party before Peter went away.

It was the old lady who directed her attention to this girl with a whisper.

"My dear Pat! Who is that *very* fashionable young person? I don't think I have often seen anything so up-to-date."

It was the right word. The girl was attired in the height of the mode. An expert only could have given the cost of her clothes, of her marvellous pochette, of her hat; particularly of a very fine diamond ornament she wore.

"I see," Pat whispered back, since the girl did not see her. "Diamonds out shopping always seem to me like golf-clubs in a ball-room. One wonders why they are there."

"A ladylike young person," said Mrs Elphinstone, as she turned away, "may be! You never know nowadays, when all the geese are feathered like swans."

They were near the entrance when she spoke. Patricia looked back at the girl, saw through the glass door a chauffeur, miraculously like Hubert's, take the lady into his charge and open the door of a car.

"Probably lends it to his fiancée for shopping," said Patricia to herself. "But if he is going to share the loaves with her, I foresee heavy food bills!"

She did not see the girl again, and promptly forgot her. A few days after that Peter's first letter arrived. It was not a diary and it was not long.

They were leaving Kilindini that day. He had loved Mombasa. It was a beautiful place, and he had been surprised to find that land there sold for about twenty times as much an acre as he could get for his best farms at home. "Fancy finding high prices in what one imagined to be a wilderness!" he wrote.

He was pleased with Townard. Mrs Gores had been a brick. She had not been sea-sick for an hour, and neither had he. Privately, he thought the going out had excited her rather. It might be the prospect of seeing where her husband was buried. Gores, in his opinion, must have been a man in a million, the way she talked of him. His memory was very green still with her.

Patricia smiled and could not say why she smiled. Peter went on to say that they had met some topping people in Mombasa.

138

A fellow there called Marshall had given him heaps of tips, and taken a snapshot of the party when they were sitting on the verandah of the hotel.

"I am bucked at the idea of going into the blue, but I must say I envy the man who stayed at home," he wound up, and she wondered if this were a reference to Hubert. "Still, I felt I must stick to the plan when I found Mrs Gores depended so much on a decision. By the way, we have taken out licences, and hope to step off on the way, as our American friends put it, before we plunge into the real business and the real bush. I'll get you a nice 'head' for your office if I can."

He ended with regards to the Elphinstones. Patricia put away his letter. She tried to think what it would be like. The start at dawn, the loads piled and ready for distribution, the scramble among the porters for easy ones. Then the town left behind, and a single file line straggling down narrow game-paths, with trees to either side, trees covered with creepers and parasites, shutting out light and air, creepers and lianas crawling underfoot, an atmosphere heavy with heat and decay. Then she laughed.

She had forgotten that they were going a long way by rail first. She had looked it up. Peter had told her they would use the Uganda railway for many miles. Instead of the start at dawn, and the winding game-paths there would be comfortable carriages on a steel rail, dinner and other meals. Her imagination had outrun Peter's progress.

The day after Peter's letter came Inspector Hoe. He came in the evening to her little flat, and accepted a cigarette.

"I suppose you thought I had got lost, miss," he said presently. "But here I am, as large as life."

He looked down at his own spreading figure, and chuckled.

"You look pleased enough to have found something," she said.

"Heard something, miss. You remember I cabled out for information about the African experiences of Mr Hanaper, or Lepper? We heard this morning that Mr Hanaper is a crook all right."

Patricia nodded. "Was one."

He grinned. "That's so. But here we are. His right name was Williams, the one he was pulled in when the confidence case came on. He started as an employé in a Kimberley diamond mine, and flew when they found he was helping the Negroes to pass out stones."

"A difficult job, I should think."

"Nowadays, I believe it is. Then a man calling himself Lepper turned up in Nairobi and got a post as a government clerk. He stayed six months, and then hurried away. When he had gone, they found he had forged a signature of some big bug. Then he vanished altogether; they don't know how. But the dates seem to make that getaway a trip home."

"So he was a forger too?" said Patricia, who had suspected it before.

"A regular rascal with some brains, miss. But it does show us that, buffalo or no buffalo, Mr Hanaper-Lepper was the kind of man to polish off Mr Gores, to cover up his steal, and it shows us that he could forge his own name to a document."

"Absolutely," said Patricia. "I quite agree with you that he murdered poor Mr Gores, directly or indirectly. The more I think of it, the more plain that seems."

Hoe finished his cigarette, and smiled again. "Nothing like having a double-barrelled gun, miss. While the people out there were hunting Hanaper's old scent, we were busy tracing Trevor from that cottage near Ceorpham."

"That's splendid! Any luck?"

"Yes, and of the kind that makes us hope we shall be able to trace all his subsequent steps. You see, once he had stayed some months near the village, and no one had worried him, he must have thought he was all right. No doubt he made some small alterations in his appearance, and felt able to think out a new campaign. So far as we can be sure of anything, we know that he went to Perth. A sporting laird there tells the tale of a man who chummed up with him, and talked of a scheme for skinning the bookies—a new system of racing bets. But the laird was a shot, not a racing-man, and he turned it down. What I hear of the scheme convinces me that it was just the sort of stuff a confidence man would put up."

"And from Perth?" she asked.

"Well, our fellows are just on that line now. I will let you hear when we get another stage."

Patricia told him then of her visit to the Belgian, and his views on big-game hunting. Hoe looked hard at her for a moment or two, and then asked a question.

"There's something at the back of your mind, miss. I wonder what it is. You didn't go to that gentleman for nothing, did you?"

"No, of course not. When I heard the kind of man Hanaper was, and knew that he had been out with Mr Gores, I wondered if he had not had a hand in the death."

"That was what we talked of. You knew I thought Hanaper had invented the buffalo."

"It wasn't the buffalo, but the misfire that worried me," protested Patricia. "Buffaloes do exist, and Mr Gores may have followed one up."

Hoe nodded, and looked interested. "I see. I see. Yes, that may be it. I may have been wide of the mark."

She stared at him. "What? I am quite off the mark, for I don't know what could have happened, Inspector. I merely wondered about it."

Hoe drummed his fingers on her desk. "Here we have a real expert's views. I may know a bit more about firearms than you, miss, but I am not up in sporting abroad. You may have given me something to go on."

"I'm glad if I have—but have I?"

He pursed his lips. "What that Belgian gentleman said was this: the hunter has a native gun-bearer with his spare gun. But he won't surely go empty-handed. No, he has another rifle; perhaps of lighter calibre, with the heavy one in reserve."

"I understood so from M de Villegaile."

"Quite. Now I don't see that Mr Gores would always have a native gun-bearer with him, unless he was actually out for the sole purpose of hunting. Suppose he is told by some Negroes that a wounded animal is lying up near a path they use. He may go out with Lepper, carrying one rifle, supported by the other. The buffalo charges him. But we don't hear that he fired the rifle he had, only that he was handed the heavy rifle, which misfired. Did he go into the game-path, knowing what buffaloes were, with empty hands?"

"It seems unlikely."

"But with Lepper close up, and knowing that a light rifle will not stop a heavy beast at close quarters, he may have reached back, after dropping the other weapon."

"That is more probable."

Hoe narrowed his eyes. "And there we have something to think over. Lepper was obviously acting as temporary gun-bearer. He was behind Gores, he had charge of the heavy rifle. What was there to prevent him from slipping out the shells Gores had loaded it with, and slipping two others into the breach?—There were six gone out of the box of ammunition you showed me."

"But why should he return that ammunition at all?"

"Perhaps because he thought the receiver would have the ammunition examined to see if it was defective. It is actually what we did do."

Patricia was full of eagerness now. "And it would be found quite serviceable?"

"Yes. He was clever enough for that, I imagine, miss."

"The only thing that I cannot understand is what he did with the shells?" she murmured.

"I know enough about rifles to explain that, miss. There are several things he could have done. You noticed that the cartridges are drawn brass. Now, men who are in the wilds have no shops to visit. Even wild-fowlers here have little machines for recharging brass cartridge-cases. What was to prevent Hanaper from taking two shells that had been fired, forcing out the caps, and recapping them? He could fix caps without a detonating substance, or with a substance which he had contrived to

142

make ineffective. There would be the cordite, and the bullet, apparently a perfectly good shell, but when the hammer fell there would be no explosion. Gores would be at the mercy of the buffalo, Hanaper could snatch up the light rifle and run. If a buffalo is anything like a bull here, he would stand and wreak his vengeance on the man he had downed."

Patricia's face flamed with indignation. "But that was murder; buffalo or no buffalo!"

"Of course. Then, miss, there was another way. What was to prevent him from drawing the bullet and the cordite, substituting twigs cut into lengths for the explosive charge, so that, even if the cap fired, the explosion did not follow? I believe you have put us on the track of the mystery."

"Beastly!" she said, frowning.

He looked grim. "You see, Gores would no doubt have talked to Lepper about the concession, told him how rich it was likely to be, and confirmed his views that his intended victim was on to a good thing. The papers were ready. It only remained to get Gores out of the way in a manner that would not arouse talk or suspicion, and clear for home with the loot."

Patricia nodded. "Then he came to me as an innocent to be fooled, and I let in Mr Carey."

"I think so. That is my opinion now. He packed up Mr Gores' belongings and sent them to the widow, with an account of the accident, and the box of ammunition. There would be nothing in the theory but for the fact that we know the kind of man Hanaper was, and also that he was in possession of Gores' papers. What a pity we didn't get our claws on Hanaper before his mate shot him."

Patricia looked doubtful. "After all, you might not have got a verdict, while we know that his accomplice made no mistake. It was an execution of sorts."

Hoe rose. "You're right, miss. Now if we can only get Mr Trevor, we complete the bag.

CHAPTER 19 A SNAPSHOT

Three days later Patricia went to tea with Mrs Elphinstone. Mr Elphinstone was out, but Hubert Gage-Chipnell was there, and greeted her with some warmth.

"I had to come to explain my long absence," he said. "Thank heaven, my sick partners have been aroused to a sense of their duty. Alone I had to fight wild barristers, whom we were instructing, and renew my youthful memories of conveyances. But Mrs Elphinstone has forgiven me, and I am happy again."

Mrs Elphinstone shook her finger at him. "Mr Gage-Chipnell has not told you the whole truth," she remarked. "Actually, he has come in to say Hail and Farewell all in one."

"Are you really going away?" Patricia asked him, laughing.

Hubert grinned. "Not so far away, nor for all time, Miss Repton. The facts are these. I have borne the heat and burden of the day for some weeks, and positively need a rest."

"So that he is going to recruit on the green sward of some quiet English village," said the old lady.

"Mrs Elphinstone wilfully misunderstands me," he said, with a smile at his hostess. "The green cloth at Monte is what she means to say. Three weeks on the Riviera will work wonders."

Patricia took the cup of tea he handed her. "Perhaps you will break the bank. Je vous en souhaite, monsieur."

"Thank you," said he. "I have no infallible system, so I may really win a little. Chance is too coquettish a goddess to like being besieged by mathematicians. Throw away your system and take your chance is her cry."

"And how soon the goddess gets tired of you," remarked the old lady.

Patricia smiled about her. "Have you heard from your cousin lately?" she asked Hubert.

"Two days ago," he said. "He was going to start the journey proper. How I envy him; with his chances of millionairedom, and a gorgeous trip in the wilds! My trip to Monte will seem a horrid anti-climax."

"Where are you staying?" Mrs Elphinstone asked.

"It depends on my friends," said he. "They can never make up their minds till the last moment."

Patricia stayed for a little after he had left. "You see how wrong you were!" she told the old lady gaily. "Mr Gage-Chipnell deserts me for the goddess of chance. Another matrimonial opening gone. I shall have to advertise soon for an eligible young man."

"African and Colonial papers please copy!"

Patricia actually flushed. "Poor Mr Carey! How his ears must tingle!"

"But how pleasurably!" cried Mrs Elphinstone. "The ears are happy that only itch with distant praises.—You didn't tell us if you had heard since, my dear."

Patricia laughed again. "Ah, I thought that was a secret. But you will be glad to hear that Mrs Gores is behaving beautifully."

"I think most women would behave beautifully to Mr Carey."

"Do you? I am not so sure," said Patricia. "Where is Mr Elphinstone today?"

"He has gone over to see Mr Everall's new find of Chinese ceramics, my dear. Yesterday he was saying how little of you he had seen lately."

"I have been busy in some ways. But I am beginning to fear that I shall never be a great figure in the city."

"You will do well in the church," said Mrs Elphinstone. "But it isn't fair to tease you, and that time is not yet.—Do come oftener. We can't have you deserting us altogether."

The next week found Patricia really busy with her grease-eliminating gadget. She had found a firm who professed themselves ready to consider its merits, and was doing her best to cheer the heart of its encouraged inventor.

Hoe did not come again, and the subject of Tom Gores' death was elbowed out of her mind for the moment.

Only Peter Carey stuck there somehow, never quite out of the picture, obstinately as was his habit, until he occupied a niche from which she never tried to oust him. He belonged there and had his place, even if she did not admit that she was in love with him.

It almost seemed that Peter Carey was in the same delicate position, for another letter came from him a week later. It was not a fragment of a diary—perhaps he had forgotten his resolution—but it contained some surprising news.

"It never seems to have occurred to me," he wrote, *"that things like Gores' affair might be registered out here."*

Patricia smiled to herself as she read. This had not occurred to her either, but Peter might be gallantly refraining from saying so.

"Here we were, nine hundred miles from the coast, blissfully pushing on to know something I could have discovered, I believe, two or three days ago. Mrs Gores and I have laughed over our ignorance, but it was a laugh that we did not mind indulging in. Here we ran against a district commissioner who knew poor Pulter well. He is just setting out for a tour of his district, but promised, the moment he knew what we were up to, to see if there was any record at headquarters of the Bangele concession.

"As to the possibilities of copper there, he says there is no doubt whatever. The copper sulphides or something have stunted or destroyed a good deal of vegetation, and trees. I am not enough of a mineralogist to follow his talk of shales and sedimentary rock, though I have heard of malachite, but what he has said is enough to convince me that Gores did know his job, and hit on a very promising

bit of land. We are going to stay here three days for our first hunt, while this DC makes enquiries."

Peter had broken off his letter there, but resumed later:

"Since I wrote last, we have heard the good news. Whether the fellow Hanaper hoped to pass off the proposition on someone who would not make enquiries on this side, or did not know Pulter's procedure, does not matter much now. It appears that Pulter got Gores to supply him with duplicate copies of the papers, and sent off a runner with them two days before he was killed in the elephant pit. Gores probably knew that he would have to register, but of course his wife did not.

"At all events, the runner got through all right, and the DC here assures us that the concession is registered in Tom Gores' name, witnessed by the late Mr Pulter. Now what follows? Am I the owner, having bought from Hanaper, who had no right to sell? It is funny, isn't it? Of course Mrs Gores and I have made an arrangement which squares matters, so that neither she nor I lose by this discovery. Only one thing is different; my anxiety to push up there as fast as possible has abated. As I told you in my last, I was pushing on then more for Mrs Gores' sake than my own, but, since she is undoubtedly the concessionaire now, an interview with the ceding chief is of no importance."

Patricia bit her lip. It looked, it really looked, as if Peter were coming home. Then she read on:

"Mrs Gores agrees that there is no necessity for it now. You will remember that Gores in his last letter spoke of a Belgian to whom he intended to put the proposition. Well, he has a survey party going up country now—not to Bangele, but five hundred miles south of it. His show is affiliated to some British copper interests in Northern Rhodesia, and would be well placed for exploiting the new area. Mrs Gores is interviewing their chief agent tomorrow, and asking them to confirm her husband's report. If they are willing to come in on a profit-sharing basis, she and I will be well pleased. They have the money, the men, the plant, all of which would take donkeys-years to *collect at home, unless one was in the financial swim. Mrs Gores and I would take vendor's shares willingly; as I can stake Mrs G till the thing is in full order.*

"Now you will be wondering what I do next. Here is the scheme. We are near fine game country, and we both want to have a try for a few trophies. Townard has planned out a trip, which will occupy us about a month, and then I am coming home. I like this country; it is all jolly interesting, and the scenery is magnificent, but, somehow, I don't think I care to carry on here just yet. I miss old England, you know. I expect you will laugh at me for what the Americans call a 'quitter', but really we have done all we came out to do, at a great deal less expense, and a hunt will round off our experiences.

"Townard I can't say too much for. He is a sportsman and a gentleman; does not mind any trouble, and has thoroughly justified himself."

Patricia sat smiling at the letter when she had finished it. Peter said something between the lines of his letter. She knew now that she was definitely glad. She wanted to see him again. She wanted it a great deal more than she would have cared to admit.

He would be on that trip now, for the letter was dated weeks back. Indeed, the hunting expedition might be almost over now, and the two of them on their way to railhead. After that would come the journey to the coast, and then home.

"I am an extraordinary creature," Patricia cried to herself when her musings took her thus far. "I might be in love with Peter Carey!"

She ran off however to tell the Elphinstones about it, and they took her eagerness for signs of the same sentimental malady, whatever she herself might have thought about it. For once, Mrs Elphinstone did not chaff her about her young man.

"But did you not know about this registration, Patricia?" asked Mr Elphinstone.

She laughed. "No, I was handicapped by a defective education. I have read a good deal of law since I first thought of my present venture, but I had an idea that the wilds of the earth had no laws.

The established protectorates and mandates I thought might have, but Mr Gores' concession was far away from the outposts."

Mr Elphinstone nodded. "You sinned in good company, Patricia, if I may call myself that, for I confess that my ideas of prospecting were (perhaps remain,) sketchy in the extreme. But, dear me, I did understand Mr Carey to say that he thought of settling out there, and now you tell us he is coming home."

"Isn't it odd!" cried his wife, with a twinkle at Patricia.

"Very strange indeed," commented the old gentleman. "I had an impression that he was a determined young man who knew his own mind."

"No man does, and very few women—that is, for more than a week at a time," said the old lady. "Well, I wish him good hunting."

Patricia smiled. "He's had it! How many concession hunters come home with a sheaf under their arm? They have really been gorgeously successful, and I am particularly glad for Mrs Gores' sake."

"And I," said Mr Elphinstone. "I admired her fortitude and resolution. I am extremely gratified to know that this will place her in a sound financial position."

The next African mail brought another letter to Patricia, but she opened it with some trepidation, for it was addressed in a hand that she did not know. Was Peter ill? Had he been hurt? She breathed a sigh of real relief when she saw that the letter was headed 'Mombasa', and contained something between two thin card slips. It was signed 'Frederick Marshall.'

"I promised a friend of yours, Mr Carey," began this innocuous epistle, *"to send you a couple of snaps I took of him and his party when he was here. If it has been delayed it is because I was down with a bout of fever, with complications.*

"You may notice that the first snap caught most of the sitters unprepared; that is the reason why Mrs Gores' head is a bit hazy. She moved it at the moment of exposure. But I expect you will recognise your friends easily enough."

Patricia eagerly surveyed the photographs. Five people sat in a row in long chairs. One to the extreme right and one to the extreme left might be guests at the hotel, but there was Peter, turning a little to speak to Mrs Gores, and the man at Mrs Gores' side laughing with a pleasant looking lady to his left. That was the first snap. The second showed them all apparently glancing straight at the wielder of the camera. Peter was grinning slightly, the man beyond Mrs Gores wore a faint frown, perhaps due to the sunlight.

Patricia turned over the card. Something was written there in a thin, angular hand:

Mr Gard, Mr Carey, Mrs Gores, Mr Townard, Mrs Marshall.

Patricia turned the photograph again. So the lady was Mr Marshall's wife, while Mr Gard was a guest. Next to Mrs Marshall, the man with the slight frown was Townard.

Patricia looked at him with interest, slowly mingled with a slight discomfort. He was rather good-looking, but somehow she did not like him. An inexplicable aversion is the commonest thing in life, but Patricia continued to stare at him, wondering why she did not care for him, or what there was in his face to justify dislike. Peter had talked of him as a sportsman and a gentleman.

No; there was nothing repellent in the face. He had a good nose, frank eyes, an agreeable mouth, and one of those chins that some dislike intensely and some admire greatly: a chin with a cleft in it.

The cells of memory function strangely, and sometimes mislead. How often do we say, 'I have seen that face before,' when the truth is that we have seen faces like it, or with some common feature.

"If I had really seen him once and disliked him, I should remember his face," Patricia said to herself, uncomfortably. "It's funny how we remember those we dislike, much more than those we like."

She looked at Peter again. He appeared to be hard and fit. She remembered that faint grin of his, more fascinating than any grin ought to be, good natured and not at all sardonic, the grin of a grown-up boy.

But her eyes went back to the counterfeit presentment of Townard, though the most prolonged scrutiny did not help her to place him.

She locked away the letter and snapshots, and went on with her business. Her latest client's contract was to he signed that day, and she was expecting him at any minute with his lawyer. It wouldn't do to be found staring at the portrait of a young man.

That evening she was dining with some friends at Kensington, and going on to a concert at Chelsea Town Hall. She came home at eleven and tumbled into bed.

She woke early next morning, and lay on her back staring up at the ceiling, pleasurably putting her lazy faculties out to grass. Her mind wandered hither and thither aimlessly, her thoughts concentrated on nothing in particular. The warm sunlight streaming into the room excited a bluebottle on the pane and made it strident and vigorous.

And then a wandering thought lighted for a moment on something tangible, unbelievable but tangible, and startled her into jumping up.

"It's Trevor!" she said to herself with dismay. "*Trevor!* But it can't be. It's quite impossible!"

But now her visual memory was wide awake, and refused to be denied. It was Trevor; the man who had looked up at her out of the photograph handed to her by Inspector Hoe!

CHAPTER 20 THE GREAT FEAR

Patricia bathed and dressed very hastily that morning. She was nervous, apprehensive, her reason fought with her memory over the identification.

How could Townard be the ruffian who had, according to Inspector Hoe's theory, shot Hanaper; the man who lived by swindling and trickery? There was enough difference between the two photographs she had seen to make her suspect that there might still be some mistake.

Yet she was afraid. The man, now she thought of it, had lived in Africa, as Hanaper had done. He had left London after Hanaper's death.

She shivered a little. She cast back over the events of those past months. Yes, there might be something in it, enough to frighten a friend of Peter Carey's. Wasn't it Townard who had asked Peter to let him go ahead to make preparations? There was no doubt of that. The man who killed Hanaper would wish, too, to get away.

But Hubert had known him, thought Patricia, and then corrected herself. Hubert did not really know him. He had met him once at a hotel somewhere, and they had chummed up. He had seen him again at a restaurant, and Townard had renewed the acquaintance.

Patricia saw in that line of conduct a confirmation of her fears. Why, that was the very characteristic behaviour of a confidence trickster. There were always the fine clothes and the air of leisured ease, the easy friendship, the subtle lead-up. The swindler made friends when and where he could. If they seemed confiding and easy to rook, a plan was evolved and a campaign inaugurated.

Hubert would not be likely, for all his good-nature, to impress a confidence-man as an innocent abroad, but there was no proof that he had tried to trick Hubert then. By the time he had come to London he was probably on the track of Peter Carey, discovered that Gage-Chipnell was Peter's cousin, and began that account of his African experiences that finally led to a recommendation to the rich young man. It all hung together disastrously.

Peter had taken a large sum of money with him, that was certain. She shivered again when she thought of that. Peter, with his money, in the hands of the man who had come out of an English jail and murdered a treacherous accomplice! The idea was terrifying. Townard had arranged a hunting trip to last a month. The party would be in the wilds!

Where had Hubert met that man? Perth. That was it, Perth!

Light flooded into her mind. Hoe had traced Trevor to Perth. She remembered that clearly. He had lost him there, but the police would be busy now, tracking Trevor's last stages of the pilgrimage south. What was she to do?

She drank a cup of coffee but did not eat. She dressed for the street. As she put on her hat she was shocked at the reflection of her face in the mirror. Her eyes were staring in an unusual way, her face was haggard.

"I ought to see Inspector Hoe at once," she said to herself as she opened the door.

She found a taxi and went to Scotland Yard. There she heard that Hoe was away, would be away for a week on holiday. They had been told that it was a walking tour. She did not tell the official who interviewed her what she thought, but scribbled a note for Hoe and asked that it should be forwarded at once.

After that, she found herself walking rather aimlessly about the streets, looking into shop windows that seemed blank. A great fear was on her. The hunting trip would be over now, but how had it ended for Peter Carey? When would she know? It was unlikely that Peter had given her name and address to anyone out there. Mrs Gores, of course, might write, or cable . . . Could she cable from the bush?

Patricia pulled herself together, and made for a cable office. She cabled to Peter at railhead, where he had last been, telling him he was wanted at home urgently. What else could she cable? To say that Townard was Trevor would mean nothing to him. To tell him that he was in danger would seem meaningless.

For a few moments she thought of cabling also to the official out there, telling him that Trevor was wanted on a charge of murder at home. But who would pay any attention to a message of that kind, coming from an unknown woman? And suppose she were wrong? Suppose Trevor was not Townard? It was too serious a matter to treat lightly.

She went out again feeling that her action had been futile. If Trevor was Townard, and that trip hunting in the bush was the basis of his plan, Peter was in danger *now*. And Peter would be in the bush; Peter and Mrs Gores.

A thought struck her and she surprised a patient official at Scotland Yard by arriving once more in his office and asking if they had the photograph of Trevor who had been convicted of working the confidence-trick.

"I know Inspector Hoe had it," she said.

"I'll make inquiries," said the official, looking at her curiously.

He came back very soon. "Inspector Hoe still has it," he said.

"But I thought he was on holiday."

"So he is, madam, but I have here a printed reproduction which has been circulated round our people in the country. I should like however to know why you wish to see it."

Patricia shrugged impatiently. "Inspector Hoe showed it to me. He—he thought I might recognise it."

"Do you?"

Patricia frowned. "I don't know. I have seen a man who may be Trevor."

"Indeed? Well, madam, we have nothing definite against Mr Trevor, as he called himself, but it would be interesting to know where you think you saw him."

"He was in Africa, if it is he."

"You have just come from there?"

"No, no. I have seen a photograph."

It was obvious that Inspector Hoe had kept his own counsel, as far as his ordinary colleagues were concerned, if this man did not know the serious suspicion that rested on Trevor.

"May I have the reproduction?" she added.

He handed her a newspaper reproduction of the photograph. "I can show you in to one of our chiefs, if you have any information to communicate," he said.

"I have nothing to communicate yet," she said impatiently. "If I have, Inspector Hoe shall hear it. Thank you for this."

She got away again, leaving the man very puzzled. When she was in the street, she took a taxi again and drove to her office. She entered her own sanctum by the side door, unlocked the drawer in which she had put the snapshots, and took them to her desk.

She laid down the flimsy reproduction side by side with the snapshot, and studied Townard's face again. In the older one he wore tiny Spanish whiskers, though he was otherwise clean-shaven. His hair was worn long, and parted in the middle. In the snapshot the tiny whiskers had gone, and his hair was cut short and parted at the side.

But, comparing each feature closely in the two portraits, there was no longer any doubt in her mind. The man on the verandah of the hotel was Trevor.

She sat up, her hands resting on the desk before her. She was trembling now pitiably. She knew that she loved Peter Carey; that she had loved him from the first week of their friendship. She was no longer concerned to deny it even to herself.

"Oh, Peter, my dear," she cried to herself despairingly, "it was I who sent you out there!"

The thought of the situation froze her blood. What could

Trevor, swindler and murderer, want with Peter Carey? Why had he schemed and intrigued to go with him? 'Glad to go for ten a month and his keep,' Hubert had been told. If Townard was indeed Trevor, what irony was in that phrase, how the man must have smiled to himself as he said it!

She dared not dwell on the thought that already a tragedy might have been consummated. She could not assure herself that the presence of Mrs Gores spelt safety for Peter. Trevor was too cunning to commit himself to any overt act. Trained in trickery, a professional criminal, he would find ways and means, as his late accomplice Hanaper had done.

Hanaper! Patricia started. Why, the very way of these men was the old way, the same confidence trick played out on the same lines, and rarely unsuccessful, though so old. And Townard would not know that he had been identified as Trevor, he would feel safe. He would not know that Hoe, or Patricia, whom he had not met, had formed a theory about Tom Gores' death. No doubt he had heard from Hanaper of the manner of that death, the means by which it had been accomplished.

The confidence trick, with its story of a benevolent donor, its dropped wallet, and the third man who always turned up to make two apparent strangers acquainted, succeeded because of its simplicity. Hanaper's trick had succeeded, and his accomplice Trevor would not scoff at it because it had been tried before. The value of a tool is its utility, and the value of a trick lies in its success.

The hunting trip which would take the whole party away from the outposts of civilisation, the presence of Mrs Gores, a witness to the apparent accidental nature of the death, these things would be accessories to Trevor's plot. She shuddered. What was she to do?

Within that month's trip, now perhaps over, lay Trevor's possibilities of mischief. But, surely, if anything had happened to Peter she would have had a cable? Then she remembered that the safari might be days away from railhead, from cable facilities. She might have to wait a week, two weeks, before she heard.

She lumped up and went blindly out of the office. She jumped into the first taxi she saw in the street below, and drove to Hubert's flat in Jermyn Street. She did not know what he could do, but he ought to be told.

But there was no one in the flat. Hubert had given his two servants a holiday, and his chauffeur had gone with him in the car. Patricia had asked her driver to wait. She came down again, and went to the office of his firm in Bond Street. They had an office there, and another in the City.

The senior partner, a mild-looking man of middle age, gave her what information he could.

"Mr Gage-Chipnell is, I understand, touring on the Riviera," he said. "He was driving to Cannes first, but I think he hoped eventually to get as far as Rapallo. Unfortunately he did not tell us how long he would stay at Cannes."

"Do you know what hotel he went to there?" she asked.

"The Splendide, I think, Miss Repton. Possibly if you wrote there they could tell you where he went on leaving. If you leave your address with me, and we hear from him, I shall have much pleasure in letting you know."

"I wished to see him with regard to his cousin Mr Carey," she said, rising. "I was the agent for the sale of a concession Mr Carey bought."

"Ah, I remember hearing it mentioned," said the lawyer, wondering why the girl looked so white and ill-at-ease. "Well, you may be sure we shall let you know at once, the moment we hear."

Where to go next, she asked herself when she had left the office. If she could only see Inspector Hoe, tell him what she had discovered, and get his advice.

Then her heart sank. What could even the Inspector do in this case, thousands of miles away from the possible scene of the disaster, where the writs of the law might not run, or run, if at all, on slow feet?

She went back to her office, consumed with miserable

thoughts. She tried to believe that there might be some hope. Suppose Trevor had at last realised that his criminal life was too dangerous to pursue further, had decided to retire on the accumulated loot before things got too hot for him. That term of imprisonment might have been a warning. It made him a marked man. A detective seeing him in one of his former West-End rendezvous would at once fasten on him, shadow him, interfere to snatch away a possible victim.

Was that likely? She shook her head. Trevor, if they were right, had risked his neck to kill the ally who had double-crossed him. He was therefore daring, unrepentant, unscrupulous. While he was getting into Hubert's confidence, he was planning to punish Hanaper; waiting to sail with Peter Carey, he had not forgotten to avenge himself on the traitor.

"Ten a month and his keep!" Why, any man with Trevor's brains could earn that at any job. The thing seemed clear enough. He had got wind of Peter's wealth, and arranged to be with Peter in the scene most suited to an ugly deed, and an easy escape. Like billiard professionals who play for the leave, not the mere stroke, the criminal plans to do his job and get away with it.

Patricia went home early. She did not know how she got through the rest of that day. She could not rest or read, and when she went to bed she lay sleepless, turning over and over in her mind a hundred dreadful possibilities.

She saw Peter Carey out there, with Townard at his elbow. A beast sprang, a rifle was raised, the breech flung open a moment later, when only two dull clicks had followed the pull of the trigger. But before two fresh cartridges could be slammed home, the beast was on Peter, and he was down.

She shut her eyes in an agony of imagination. Tom Gores had died like that, but surely not Peter!

But Trevor was ruthless, as Hanaper had been ruthless. He must have been the man who had kneeled calmly by a chair in the dark room in that house at Willesden, staring into the lighted room beyond, coolly and accurately levelling his revolver at the head of the man who had once worked with him, pulling a quick trigger with the sangfroid and the deadly accuracy of a shot at target practice.

Patricia shivered violently, and burst into a torrent of sobs. The light crept grey into the room to find her still awake.

CHAPTER 21 WAITING

Patricia's first thought as she rose was to go to her friends the Elphinstones. But what could she tell them? The secondary horror of her ordeal was the futility of any effort. Had Peter been in the British Isles, even in Europe, she could have been sure of reaching him by wire; she could have warned the police and had help sent. But in Africa the vast spaces defeated her.

Her cable would have been received by now, she thought. But what was the procedure? Would the people at the other end send a runner after the safari, and, if so, did they know to within two hundred miles where the safari would be? A hunting expedition there could not be like an ordered grouse-drive or pheasant-shoot, where the butts and beats are decided beforehand, and lunch is provided at a fixed spot. Natives might come in with news of game at a distance, a tracker might take them into the bush after buffalo or elephant. Man proposes, but game disposes, is the word in such hunting.

Patricia's mind was always with Peter now. Sometimes she saw him alert and vigorous, miraculously preserved from the net spread to entangle him; again she saw him dead, or dying, the victim of some savage beast, at its worst less savage than the man who had stood at Peter's side.

She did not go into the office at all that day but telephoned Miss Froud to carry on. At lunch time she looked for Dick Caley, and shocked him by her appearance. She had tried to wipe out, and powder over, the ravages of her tears in the night, but Caley could not fail to see that something had profoundly moved her.

"Why, you look a regular wreck, old thing," he said

solicitously, "Not ill, are you?"

"I am rather anxious," said Patricia.

"Anxious! My dear girl, you look all in. What the dickens is the matter? Can I help?"

Patricia had known him many years, and she plunged. "Dick, I told you a friend of mine has gone out to Africa. He is on a shooting trip, and I have a horrid feeling that something has happened to him."

Caley looked at her sharply. Why, Patricia was in love with someone at last, this merchant she had talked of before, the fellow who had bought that concession at Bang-something-other!

"Why, what an idea!" he smiled to reassure her. "You don't know, but you have a horrid feeling? Don't let that worry you, my dear. I have had lots of horrid feelings about people, but they never came to anything. Hunting? Why, lots of chaps go out and get their lion or two, and never turn a hair. I believe Mr Lion is a bit of a holy humbug, gets up his hackles, and roars, and looks majestic, just to keep his spirits up. Besides, your pal will have his hunter with him, and dollops of armed natives."

"It's his hunter I'm worrying about," she murmured.

He produced a cigarette-case, and gave her a cigarette. "I advise you to try a gasper to settle your nerves a bit. Let's have this out. The hunter? Well, I never heard you had been out there. What can the Negro represent to you? They're not all savages, you know."

"But he isn't a Negro," she said; "he is a man who was engaged by Peter Carey here."

"What of that?"

She hesitated. "Well, I have proof—a sort of proof—that he is a rogue. That is why I am so nervous and anxious."

He started. "Good heavens! But are you sure of your proof? And, after all, a rogue isn't necessarily a murderer—most aren't. —Is your Mr Carey alone?"

"A lady Mrs Gores is with him too."

Dick stared. "A friend, I suppose?"

"A friend of mine too."

"Then what is your worry? Rogues don't want witnesses."

Patricia shrugged. "Never mind. I have the feeling and I can't get rid of it. Will you do something for me?"

"I, old girl! Can you ask?"

"Then I want you to see your friend in the Colonial Office at once. I want someone to get hold of Mr Carey and make him come home. I cabled yesterday to the railhead, but I don't know if they will deliver the cable. They may think it must wait till he returns from that hunting trip. I suppose your friend knows if some official out there could be warned directly."

"I'll ask him, when I leave you, and telephone the news on," said Dick, making a note on his cuff. "Let me see now. There is a Mr Carey. What did you say the name of this hunter is?"

"He calls himself Townard."

"Right. Mr Carey, Mr Townard, a Mrs Gores. Left railhead Uganda railway for hunting trip."

"You might say that they had been in touch with the District Commissioner there. They made enquiries from him about the Bangele concession."

"Good egg! This DC may be the very fellow to cable. He will have extensive powers and lots of men at his disposal. My pal Gunter is only one of the young things at the office, but his guv'nor is way high up. We'll put this through for you."

"I'm awfully grateful to you, Dick," she said.

"Don't be! Look here, old thing, I'm not going to condole with you, but to congratulate you, see? Mr Peter Carey is probably as well as you are, and he is a very lucky devil. If this other chappie is a rogue, he probably joined up to get out of the country under a respectable wing.—But I'll see Gunter at once."

His cheerfulness, even his rather indefinite explanation of Townard's reason for taking service under Peter, did something to restore Patricia's spirits for the time being. The Colonial Office could surely get in touch with Peter more quickly than anyone else, through its officials and agents.

She began to see the other side. Trevor, in full triumph and

162

successfully carrying on his nefarious business, might not go abroad for a bare ten pounds a month. But Trevor had more than that to think about. He had killed a man and, though no one had appeared to suspect him of it, he must have known that the police might strike his track. He had done a daring thing when he got into that house in Willesden and shot down his ally.

But this fit of optimism did not last long. Away from Dick Caley's cheerful presence, Patricia found herself sinking again into the old slough of doubt and despair.

The waiting grew intolerable. Even if the message was taken straight to Peter, days would elapse before she got an answer. She hurried to the Elphinstones' house, and turned away on the very doorstep. She was not in the mood for explanations. Her old friend would want to know everything.

She was tired and depressed. At the Polytechnic there was a cinema lecture given by some traveller. It was illustrating a big-game hunt in the Congo.

Patricia went in, paid for a seat and sat down. A lean and sunburned man was explaining a scene as she came in. Then the film flickered on. Patricia sat spellbound. Peter was out in a place like that. She saw a plain with high grass, and natives with spears advancing through it. A man, not the lecturer, was in the centre of the advancing line. He had a rifle in his hand.

The lean man on the platform raised his voice. "If you watch carefully," he said in his easy voice, "you may see how justified were the ancients when they said that something new always came out of Africa, but in hunting there is not only the new but the unexpected that usually happens. My friend is about to get a double shot at a species of antelope which is very common out there—ah, here they come——"

He broke off as a herd of antelope broke through the grass and wheeled, their curving horns laid back, their speed tremendous. Patricia saw the man with the gun fire twice; an animal to his left bounded high in the air and toppled over; a second buck, obviously hit too far back, went on, but more slowly than the rest of the herd. The voice of the lecturer was raised again.

163

"A commonplace that; but mark what follows. My friend has a quite unrehearsed and exciting moment. The antelope go, but a sleepy rhinoceros, which has lain hidden in the grass, gets up to see what is happening. You will observe that he does not like the looks of my friend—here he is!"

Patricia felt all her muscles contract as the grey lumbering beast broke cover. She saw the spearmen dart to this side and that; then the sportsman in the middle handed back his rifle to a Somali behind him, and grasped his heavy rifle.

Patricia felt for the moment paralysed and sick. The brute was coming on at a lumbering gallop. The man with the rifle, cool and collected as if he faced a mere rabbit, shouldered the butt of his gun and took careful aim.

Involuntarily, Patricia covered her eyes with a hand. She could not look. She had seen one or two of these hunting films before, but now Peter was out there, and her blood was chilled. When she looked again, the beast lay on its side, natives clustering about it, the sportsman with one foot on its head and a rather conscious air of posing for a picture. The lecturer went on:

"Surprise for surprise—a fair exchange. But unfortunately it is not always so, for human nerves are human after all, and a shot at these beasts must be well placed. . . ."

Patricia got up and stumbled out in the half light of the hall. The lecturer's words were ringing in her ears. "Unfortunately it is not always so."

It was not always so! Poor Tom Gores had proved that in the face of a more determined foe than that lumbering, purblind pachyderm. A shot ill-aimed would be enough, and worse a shot that was never fired at all.

She went home to her flat and moved restlessly about it for an hour. She wondered if Dick Caley would telephone soon. But it was six o'clock before Caley got through, to inform her that old Gunter had taken action; unofficially, of course. The District Commissioner had been asked to recall Peter if he could find him.

Patricia thought with terror of the night. The last had been sheer misery, and already her nerves were feeling the effects of that sleepless time when harassing thoughts had been her sole company.

"I wish I had never seen that beastly picture," she groaned. "I don't think I shall ever forget it now."

But she went to bed at twelve, and slept for four hours, without a dream, waking before dawn with a blank mind.

But that blankness did not last long. Peter came to take his place in the niche, and now it was an appealing Peter; Peter in danger, voicelessly crying to her for help. Before love had come to Patricia she had not known what agony was. Now she knew it, and saw everything black, every good thing taken out of her world.

She watched the darkness grow thin, struggle with the grey, and vanish. The yellow light of dawn was filtering in when she got out of bed and went to the window to draw up the blind. As she passed her mirror she caught a glimpse of her face. The skin showed sallow and ashy in that pale light, and there were black rings about her eyes. The corners of her mouth drooped. That last sign of desperate weariness and misery flogged her failing courage. She set her lips, and threw up her head. This was not the time to give in, or lower her flag.

She went into her little bath-room and turned on the water. While the bath filled she put a little kettle on a gas-ring, and set out her tray for tea.

Presently she came back and sat down, wrapped in her dressing-gown. She drank a cup of tea slowly, lighted a cigarette, and stared out of the window at the redly flushed sky.

Surely Mr Gunter would get a reply today? Unless, of course, the District Commissioner was off on one of his periodical inspections. But, in that case, a subordinate might reply. She crushed her half-smoked cigarette out on an ash-tray, and began to dress rapidly. She was wishing she could get at Hubert. Perhaps he could do no more than she, but she felt the need of someone to confide in, someone more in touch with the actual facts than the Elphinstones, who were kind but ineffectual.

She made her breakfast early, and ate something, despite a great disinclination to eat. With the arrival of the post she wakened up.

There was a postcard from Hubert Gage-Chipnell, with a charming coloured photograph of Cap Martin on the reverse. She hardly looked at the few words he had written, but glanced eagerly at the address, "Hotel Beauton, Cap Martin."

She sat down at once to write to him, telling him what she had heard, and asking him to wire advice, or, if he thought it wiser, also to cable to Peter at railhead. Then she went out to post her letter.

She came back as restless as before. It occurred to her that a letter took some days, two perhaps. She ought to have wired.

"I shall wire!" she said to herself, and sat down to fill up a flimsy she took from her writing desk. She went down to the office before Miss Froud arrived. Dick Caley would probably telephone to her there. She forgot in her agitation that the Foreign Office staff did not go to work so early. She put in the wire on her way, and felt that she had done all she could for the moment.

She remembered as she sat down in her chair the last time she had talked there with Peter Carey. It was amazing how vividly his image persisted in her memory, clear-cut as a cameo, intensely real. She ought to have known then what she felt about him, and not been afraid of it. For it was very clear today that some part of her had known, but hid the knowledge from the light.

It was absurd to protest, as her common sense did, that a woman cannot disclose her feelings. If anything had happened to Peter, she said she would never forgive herself.

CHAPTER 22
INSPECTOR HOE
CONCURS

Patricia received an astonished Miss Froud and asked her at once to take the day off. Miss Froud was grateful, but not very sure if she ought. The appearance of Patricia shocked her, and a sympathetic inquiry was on the tip of her tongue, though something unresponsive and hard in her employer's eyes checked the question before it was uttered.

"I may close the office very soon," said Patricia. "I hope you will enjoy yourself."

"You don't mean close it for good, Miss Repton?"

"I don't know. I suppose not. I meant for today. Don't trouble, please, to attend to anything. You may come in tomorrow as usual."

Miss Froud went off, shaking her head. Something was wrong, but she could not quite understand what it was. Her thoughts naturally flew back to the attractive young man who had come in about that African business; but she had seen nothing in Patricia to suggest that there was anything in the wind in that quarter.

When Patricia was alone, she tried to kill time and thought by studying that dry legal work she had once sent Miss Froud out to buy. A law book is the ideal bedside book. The interminable jargon of the law, the roundabout phrases, redundant and desiccated, stupefy the ordinary lay senses, and produce a prompt narcotic effect not paralleled elsewhere.

But nothing could keep Patricia's thoughts away from Peter and his danger, and her mind revolved round that harrowing centre endlessly.

The morning was half way through when a ring made her start and jump up. She hurried into the outer office. What was it? Was it by any chance a cable? She opened the door, and found Inspector Hoe on the threshold.

"I didn't hear anyone in, so I rang," he said. "No one heard me, and I peeped in to see. But there was no young lady here, so I went out into the passage once more. I was just going away when I thought you might be in your own office."

"Come in," said Patricia. "If you rang twice, I did not hear you."

He followed her to the inner office, and she motioned him to sit down, while she produced the two photos of Trevor.

"Look at that!" she said eagerly. "Is it Trevor—*is it?*"

He saw how haggard she looked, but made no immediate comment, as he stared from one photograph to the other.

"They told me at the Yard you had called and wished to see me," he said. "I just got back early this morning."

"Is it Trevor?" she cried, as if she had not heard him.

He was a large but not a slow man. The moment he looked down he knew what she was thinking, and why she was so moved. The seriousness of the situation broke upon him at once.

"To the best of my knowledge and belief, miss, it is," he said slowly, using the familiar term in his excitement. "By George, miss, this has done us! We had him as far as London, and he has slipped out of our fingers."

She bit her lip. "He left town a day or two—or was it three days —after Hanaper was killed?"

"After, anyway," said the detective, drumming with his fingers. "Have you done anything?"

"I have cabled to Mr Carey, but of course only to the place where he left to strike into the bush, and I have asked a gentleman in the Colonial Office to cable to the District

Commissioner out there to recall Mr Carey at once, if he can get at him. I have also wired this morning to his cousin Mr Gage-Chipnell. Trevor managed to secure his recommendation, you remember."

Hoe nodded. "I remember now. Well, I don't see that you could have done more. We, of course, will pull our strings. We can get Trevor on the charge of murdering his associate, subject, of course, to——" He paused.

"To what?" she demanded.

"Your limitations are ours, miss. We may not find it easy to have him arrested out there, even to find him quickly for a start, but we'll put the law in motion, anyway."

Patricia nodded, frowning. "You see what this may mean?"

"Well enough," he said slowly, "though in this case we'll hope we're wrong. Trevor had to get away, and he laid his train to get away most easily."

She shrugged. "Just the confidence method over again. I have been telling myself that, ever since I saw the resemblance. He heard Mr Gage-Chipnell was Mr Carey's cousin, chummed up with him, and talked of his African experiences. It's the roundabout approach that makes these men so successful."

Hoe nodded. "You are on the telephone here. I'll get through at once, if you don't mind, to my chief, and ask him to expedite matters."

"Do," said Patricia.

He went into the outer office and began to speak after a few moments' wait. Patricia did not hear what he said. She was staring at the photographs absently. He returned very soon, closed the communicating door, and sat down.

"To be frank, miss, the danger is that Trevor had an ugly scheme on hand."

"I am afraid so," she said, just above her breath. "We know what happened to Mr Gores. You traced Trevor to Perth, didn't you? I remembered yesterday that Mr Gage-Chipnell met him first in a hotel there."

"Oh, it's him all right," remarked Hoe. "But where exactly does this matter stand? Mr Carey and he are on a hunting trip, and have got away from railhead, as you put it. When did they start?"

She found the letter from Peter and handed it to him silently. He read it and looked grim.

"It looks like the same kind of frame-up Hanaper played on Gores," he said presently. "Only the same trick twice might be too suspicious for him to work it."

"No," said Patricia in a dull voice. "He would not know anyone associated him with Hanaper, even with the man you know as Trevor. It would seem an accident, a coincidence if you like, but that is all. Even Mrs Gores would not understand the meaning of it, for she believes her husband was betrayed by bad ammunition, and not by his companion."

"That's true. It isn't nice hearing for you, miss, but facts have to be faced sooner or later. If Trevor planned to get Mr Carey alone in the wilds he may take some nasty action. Mr Carey must have had a good deal of money with him. On the other hand, we need not exaggerate. There is a factor in the situation now that Trevor did not count on when he set out."

"What is that?"

"The presence of Mrs Gores. That was an afterthought of Mr Carey's, you see."

"I've considered that. You may be right. He may be afraid to act while she is there, on the other hand, while there might be an allegation of foul play if they were alone, Mrs Gores provides a witness he could call on."

"You mean if he tampered with the ammunition?"

"I do."

Her voice was firmer now, and her manner more composed. When Hoe had come in, he had noticed the ravages her anxiety had made. He admired the courage which was gradually coming to her aid.

"Well, we'll face that possibility, but we won't take it for granted. Hanaper knew Gores was out after a wounded buffalo lying up in bush by the path. But Mr Carey's shoot may not include a buffalo—they aren't all over Africa, you know. Also he

170

may not come on lion or any dangerous beast. Hanaper's plan depended on a critical moment."

"But is it likely they will not meet with dangerous beasts?"

He shrugged. "I know as little as you do, miss, but I have read some accounts of hunting out there, and it seems to me men do go out for lion and see none; and others fit out for elephant and never glimpse a tusk."

"That is true," she reflected. "You give me more courage. But there is always the danger of a rifle accident, or a murder made to appear one."

"Look here, miss," said he bluntly, "we shall have enough to worry about without inventing new ideas. Our people are acting at once, you have cabled yourself, and got the gentleman in the Colonial Office to cable. We can't do more at the moment."

"But how can I wait?"

He shook his head sympathetically. "It's very hard, I know, but there you are. The District Commissioner or his man in charge is bound to reply as soon as he can. Either he will say Mr Carey has come in safely with his party or he has not. Once we know that definitely, you can begin to worry or rejoice, as the case may be. It may be good news. You never know. But if you fret yourself into a shadow in advance it won't do you any good or the gentleman either."

He rose. Patricia looked up at him.

"You are going? Can I get you at any time on the telephone?"

"If I am away I'll leave a message, miss, and get them to keep you posted," he said.

Truly he had given Patricia courage. There might be something in what he had said. Africa was the country of lions and buffaloes, but even there these beasts were not to be met with at every corner.

She telephoned Dick Caley. There was no news yet, he said, but be would ring Gunter up again. Patricia had to be content with that. She closed the office at four and went home.

But no message came that day. The suspense was growing intolerable again. She was afraid to go to the Elphinstones' for

171

fear she would give way. This was not the time for tears.

That night dragged again. Among her post there was nothing to encourage her. She went to the office as usual, but it was twelve o'clock before anyone came. Then she was surprised to find Dick Caley.

"Come straight in, Dick," she said, and he followed her and closed the door.

"A bit of news, but it may be only a rumour," he said, and looked anxious. "Gunter tells me his father got a cable from the DC out there. He's sending it round, but I thought I had better run over to tell you at once."

She moistened dry lips. "Is it bad news, Dick?"

He shrugged. "I don't know. And, as I say, the DC cables it as a native rumour. News travels fast among the Negroes."

Patricia drew a deep breath. "Tell me."

He nodded. "He said, 'natives rumour white man badly mauled by leopard. Am getting further particulars and sending out help.'"

"No name, Dick?"

"No name, old girl," he said uncomfortably.

She was very white, but though he watched her closely, he could see no other signs of faintness or loss of control.

"There were two out there," she said.

"Of course, old thing. I expect the other beggar got it in the neck. You see, your Mr Carey was the big man of the trip; t'other chap was only his hunter. Perhaps the DC would have given the name if it had been your pal."

"Possibly," said she. "Thank you for coming, Dick."

"I must really get back to the office," he said, glancing furtively at her. "But are you sure you'll be all right?"

She straightened herself. "Quite, Dick. It may be the other. You're telling the truth about this—there was no name?"

"Honest Injun, my dear! It's the gospel truth."

When he had gone Patricia leaned her head down on her hands.

But she did not cry. Her eyes were dry when she raised her

head. She felt deadly sick. Waves of it rolled over her. Her forehead was clammy and cold.

She gripped each side of her desk hard with her hands and closed her eyes again for a minute. When Dick Caley had said it might be the other man, he did not know the circumstances, who that other man was, or the horror that had happened before.

"Peter! Peter!" she kept crying to herself till it sounded like a dirge for him.

Miss Froud opened the inner door and looked in. She withdrew hastily. Patricia did not know that the door had opened and closed again quietly. She made a great effort presently, and sat up very straight, commanding her nerves, setting her teeth hard.

Peter or Townard, the ruffian Trevor? The question posed itself a thousand times, and there was no answer to it.

Hastily she took up her desk telephone and called up Inspector Hoe. Luckily he was not out, but a few minutes elapsed before he spoke to her.

"That Miss Repton? Any news?"

"Yes. A cable has come. Mr Gunter got it. It is, so far as he knows, mentioned as a native rumour, but it says one of the hunting party has been badly mauled by a leopard, and is dangerously ill. No name given."

She heard Hoe's soft whistle of surprise, then, "The kind of thing we feared, miss," he said. "But don't give up hope. It mayn't be our man. What are they doing?"

"Out there? Oh, they have sent help. That shows the party were some distance from railhead, or they would have brought the wounded man in."

"That's true, miss. But we'll hear soon. The people there are sure to send a runner back with more information, even if the gentleman can't be moved just yet. If you don't mind, miss, I'll come round to your flat this evening. I have an inquiry on hand now that I must see to."

"Anything about this?"

"In a way it is, miss. Expect me this evening."

He rang off.

CHAPTER 23 DOUBTS

Patricia's ordeal now was more trying than any she had undergone before. It was not a case now of speculating if the blow would fall. A blow had fallen, but she did not know upon whom.

She was not sure, that is, but everything told her that it was Peter. Hoe saw her that evening. He tried to reassure her by saying that at the worst Peter Carey might recover, even if it were he who had been the victim of the leopard's attack. But in the meantime she had been to see M de Vilegaille, the only man she knew who had experience of African hunting.

The Belgian had been sympathetic and evasive. But she saw from his manner that he was not very hopeful. He admitted that the ferocity, the litheness and quickness of the leopard made it one of the most dangerous beasts. He could not deny that the teeth and claws of the carnivores were liable to poison what they tore. But he was not altogether pessimistic.

"The modern safari is not the old, when one went out with only the native, with no proper medicine or antiseptic, mademoiselle. *Du tout*—not at all. Now, one has iodine and other things, and in this case you have the two white men, also a lady who has some experience with the late Monsieur Gores."

She told Hoe all this, and he nodded. "I think he's right, miss. You don't, even know when this took place. It may have been two weeks ago, and if it was that, then the gentleman must be holding his own well."

"I would give my head to know," she cried passionately.

"There's some things I'd nearly give mine to know," he said

slowly. "This is an odd case—a very odd one."

"It's horrible," she said.

He got up. "Well, keep me informed if you will, miss. I am sorry I have nothing new to tell you."

She felt that she must tell the Elphinstones now. She was surer of herself. She believed she would not break down.

Mrs Elphinstone was shocked when Patricia turned up and told the news. Her shrewd eyes saw what Patricia felt, and though she did not minimise the possible disaster, she took the line that Hoe and de Villegaile had done.

But then she knew nothing of Trevor alias Townard, and her assurances did not assure. Mr Elphinstone was away, so Pat stayed to dinner with the old lady, and then rushed back to her flat, in case a cable had come.

But none came that day or the next. Three days went by. It was on the fourth day that she found a cable awaiting her when she reached the office. She tore open the envelope, glanced at the message, and fainted dead away.

She had fallen forward on her desk, and no sound warned Miss Froud in the outer office that anything was amiss. Patricia came to within a minute, weakly grasped the sides of her desk and clung there till she felt better. Then she took the cable form from where it had fluttered into the desk and read the contents with tears running down her cheeks.

It wasn't Peter!

Her eyes ran along the lines, under which Peter Carey had signed his name.

Townard mauled leopard serious injuries plucky attempt save Mrs Gores both others safe and well
    Carey

She rose unsteadily and drank a glass of water from a carafe she kept in a cupboard. Joy flooded over her, overwhelmed her, was like a song in her heart.

Then she thought of Townard. Surely he had done something

to expiate his misdeeds in the past? Chivalry had urged him when a critical moment came. Indeed, in the light of this, it seemed possible that the man had really determined to give up his old ways. How could she say now that he had planned to kill Peter as his old associate had killed Gores? No one could say. Sometimes even the evil man repents and turns back.

She rang up Inspector Hoe once more, and told him. He congratulated her warmly, but was unexpectedly lukewarm about her theory of Townard, or Trevor's repentance.

"We can't say, miss. We had better wait to hear more."

So Patricia had to wait. But it was different waiting now. Even if Hoe proved right in his doubts, and Trevor had been robbed of an opportunity to carry out an evil plan, Peter's only enemy was past doing him a hurt.

Dick Caley came later with a cable from the District Commissioner to Mr Gunter, confirming the news, but hardly amplifying it. The wounded man was being brought in, but there was not much hope.

The days went on again. There were no more cables from Peter for a week, and then came one telling her that Townard was dead. Patricia shook her head over that. It might have been Peter.

She was waiting for a letter now. She was certain Peter would follow up his first cable by writing. But letters took a long time to come.

But now she was herself again, began once more to try to negotiate the two small propositions left on her hands, which did not promise well, but at least gave her something to do, and occupation for her restless mind. She went to the Elphinstones' regularly, and Dick Caley took her out to dances once a week. Dick had just become engaged to a girl who lived in Edinburgh, and welcomed what he called a fellow-sufferer with whom he could enthuse on the passion of love.

Dick was the only one who knew that Patricia really was in love with the absent Peter, and the only one whose good-humoured jests she did not resent.

"You see, old thing," he used to say, "we are about the only moderns who believe still that absence makes the heart grow fonder. But, being isolated, we have to comfort one another."

"You go too fast, Dick," she told him. "Speak for yourself. I don't mind consoling you, if that is what you mean."

"Hard luck he has to cool his ardour in a cable!" he said irrepressibly. "Perhaps you have a code."

All the same, the days went slowly and the weeks crawled. Patricia went down again to the offices of Hubert's firm to see Hubert. But he was still away. The senior partner had heard from him last from Aix-les-Bains, but imagined he was going south again soon.

"You see, Miss Repton," he added, "he has not been well, and as we have a French client who wanted some business done, we asked him to visit Aix and see to it. He should be home soon."

Patricia wired to the hotel at Aix but did not get an answer. Probably Hubert had gone south. At any rate it was certain that he would have heard the news from Peter.

The letter that came at last from Peter had not taken a minute longer than was necessary, but it seemed to Patricia that an age had elapsed between it and the cable. She was at home when it came, and sat down with eager eyes to read it.

I am writing this after sending you the cable about poor Townard (he wrote, and Patricia, looking at the date of his letter, understood that he must be referring to the first wire). *It has been a great shock to Mrs Gores and myself, as you may imagine. The only happy thought about it to me was that I was able to shoot the brute, and so save Townard from being killed there and then. His injuries are very severe, but he has a great deal of vitality and is wonderfully plucky, so we have not yet given up hope.*

His conduct all through has been beyond praise, but I had better explain exactly what happened, so that you may have an opportunity of judging for yourself.

The whole thing was caused in the first instance by the laziness of some of our porters, but I should have seen to it that they did their work. As you may know, a thorn hedge, or boma, is generally put up at night round the camp if there are wild beasts in the vicinity. Leopards, being great jumpers, are hard to keep out in any case, but a few of the men left a gap in the boma, as they had to go a little distance to cut thorn, and wanted to save trouble for themselves.

The second cause, I feel sure, was the monkeys. It is true we had a few sheep in the boma, and a goat or two, but those were not in the tents. Mrs Gores made pets of two monkeys some weeks ago. They were jolly little things, but having them in her tent was the trouble. Leopards are fond of monkeys, and I think the little brutes' chattering brought this one where he wasn't wanted.

But I am getting ahead of my story. Townard and I had one tent, and Mrs Gores a smaller one to herself. We had had a long day's hunting and I was absolutely done to the world. Before we turned in someone heard a lion roaring, but our fires must have warned him off, for we heard no more of him. I suppose it was about midnight, and I was sound as a top, when the very devil of a noise broke out near us. There was a snarling and screeching, Mrs Gores screamed, the infernal monkeys went wild, and all our Negroes bolted, some of them running right into the thorn hedge and sticking there like soldiers on wire.

I jumped out of bed in time to hear Townard go crashing out of the tent. But it was black as the ace of spades in there, and I collided with the tent-pole and nearly brought the show down. Then I couldn't find my rifle, and all the while there was that devilish hullabulloo, though I could not hear Mrs Gores' voice then. I don't suppose it was long, but it seemed an age before I picked up a rifle and made tracks for Mrs Gores' tent. It was down, and though she had pluckily got a torch, one could not see much but a lot of canvas jumping and wriggling about, and hear a yell or two and a continuous snarling.

About that time, a dog one of the natives owned ran butting into the fallen tent, and the leopard came out from under and stood staring at us. I put him out with a lucky shot that cut the vertebra across, and then we got to work on the torn and jumbled tent, and found poor Townard under it.

Once we had done in the leopard, the natives came running in, full of the helpfulness we didn't want, but we made them light torches, *got two hurricane lamps going, and had a look at the poor chap.*

I won't go into any of the beastly details, but he was fearfully clawed about, though quite conscious, and asking if Mrs Gores was all right and safe. He was a real man, I can tell you, I have got Mrs Gores' account of the affair, and though it is scanty it tells us what happened. It seems that she was awakened by the beastly monkeys jabbering and crying like kids. The next thing she knew the leopard had crashed into the tent and grabbed one of her pets. She promptly and with great presence of mind crawled out under the tent the other side, and then Townard must have come across before the beast had got out.

His part required no telling. I could see that he had jumped to the trouble quicker than I, though he had been sound asleep when the noise broke out, grabbed the nearest rifle (which appears to have been mine) and gone hell-for-leather to the rescue. But here comes the point, and a curious one. I heard no shots from him, and I was sure the leopard had got him before he saw it and could take aim. Not a bit of it. He had loosed off both barrels, and both had misfired!

My rifle! Do you see that? It was the one that let poor Tom Gores down so badly, and when I come home I am going to have a quiet word with the maker. It couldn't have been the cartridges, since I bought fresh ones for it before I left home, and have tested the rest of the packet since. I have packed the rotten thing with the shells in it, and it shall go to the maker with a big query marked on it. I think that fact upset Mrs Gores even more than Townard's injury, for she had sold it to me, and she knew it had been the means of causing her husband's death.

It has struck me since that I have never used the rifle here. We saw nothing that I was not able to tackle with my .297, and though Townard wanted me to strike off a day or two after elephant, I did not want to leave Mrs Gores alone in camp, and refused. How glad I am! Elephant would have required the .577, and that putrid gun would have left me cold. I am jolly glad I refused that hunt.

We are going to try to take Townard in. He seems fair so far, and the only real danger is the wounds becoming septic. We have invented a fine litter for him, and he wants us to try to make for the rail. He never confides in me, but I have an idea that he is a broken-down gentleman who has not had a very easy life. Poor chap! I hope we shall save him yet. I will see that he doesn't want for anything in the future, if we pull him through.

He is very grateful to me, though I did nothing until the trouble was done, and still more grateful to Mrs Gores. I asked him about the misfires, but he only shook his head, and said he could not remember. By the way, you might tell old Hubert all this. I did not cable him, but thought you would pass the news on. I hope he keeps fit and well. Tell him I shall strike for home at the first opportunity.

I hope you weren't worried by my cable. It occurred to me the news might get home somehow, and you might think that I had got the knock. That sounds egotistical, but you know what I mean. We were good friends, and I knew you would be interested. Well, I must get this off now, as a runner is going in, and I may not have the chance for some time again.

Patricia looked up, her eyes shining. She knew more than Peter had known, and the implication of that suggested elephant hunt and the mystery of the misfires. But Peter was safe, and that was the great thing.

"I don't think I shall ever tell him," she said to herself, as she began to read his letter for the second time.

CHAPTER 24
THE LETTER

"I can't tell you how delighted we are, Pat," said Mrs Elphinstone when she heard the latest news. "Splendid!"

"Though naturally we are distressed to hear of the death of the good fellow who accompanied him," said her husband in his precise voice; "yet, after all, a man can only die nobly. He can do no more. And that, I am sure, is the death Mr Townard would have wished to die."

Patricia skated rapidly over that thin ice. "It would have been dreadful if Mrs Gores had been killed," she commented; "but now that she has put her affairs in the hands of that Belgian company, and has escaped that brute, I expect she will come home with Peter Carey."

"Does Hubert Gage-Chipnell know?" asked Mrs Elphinstone. "He will be pleased."

"I wired to him," said Patricia, and then caught an odd look on Mr Elphinstone's face. "He's on the Riviera, I understand."

"Didn't he say he was going to Monte Carlo?" cried the old lady, taking no notice of distress signals waved by her husband. "My brother-in-law is there and he wrote to say he had seen him. From what he says I gather that Mr Gage-Chipnell must come home soon to collect some more of those loaves and fishes he told us about. Apparently he is dissipating them at a great rate."

"Really?" Patricia laughed. "So the lack of a system has not proved more profitable than the possession of one."

Mr Elphinstone frowned. "Jane ought not to have told you that. We must remember that a great many young men, whether we deprecate it or not, lose money at the tables."

His wife smiled. "My dear, didn't you say you had arranged to play in your club's veteran handicap this afternoon?"

He raised his eyebrows. "Why, so I did! Turner owes me a hundred and fifty in the game, and I think I have an excellent chance. I am sure you will excuse me, Patricia."

She nodded. "The best of luck," she said, "and confusion to Mr Turner."

When he had gone her hostess crinkled up her face in a knowing smile. "You know how he hates gossip, Pat. So do I, on the whole, but I must tell you this. My brother-in-law saw Mr Gage-Chipnell, but was not seen. He was about to go up and speak when he detected the presence of a young lady—at least, that was his trouble, for although she was young, he was not certain that she was the other thing! He is even straiter than my husband, and he managed to edge away."

Patricia's mind jumped to the girl they had seen in Harrods'. "Poor loaves and fishes!" she murmured.

Mrs Elphinstone nodded. "Both ends of the candle, my dear! My brother-in-law heard he had been there some time, playing very high, and consistently losing. Talk was beginning to spread about him and the very magnificent young woman. It was thought at first—he is dark, you know—that he was one of those South American millionaires who fling their money about."

"I'm sorry," said Patricia. "I did not know he had been long there."

"Well, he has taken a villa near at hand, my dear. Yet he might have known, even at this time of year, he would meet some people from England."

"That might account for my messages not reaching him," said Patricia. "It is true I got a postcard from a hotel at Cap Martin, but I suppose he merely took his car there for the night and went on again."

But when she left for home again she had forgotten Hubert.

She knew now that she had never thought of falling in love with him, and she was glad of it; being one of those sensible girls who are not attracted to rapid men. But it was not her affair if Hubert chose to lose his money at the tables, or create scandal by carelessly-chosen company.

A week later she had another letter from Peter Carey, and this time it struck her as at once the oddest and most precious letter conceivable. Peter began by telling her that he was on his way home, and ended by a declaration as sincere as it was clumsy and boyish.

I suppose you will think me a coward for writing this, as if I were afraid to wait until I saw you. It really isn't that. Since I realised what you meant to me, Patricia, I have worried my head off, thinking some other fellow might be with you and take you away from me before I had a chance to tell you I loved you.

No, I don't quite mean what I have written. I have no business to suggest that you looked at me in that light. Only I want to tell you now that I love you. I want you, if you will, to let me tell you this when I come back. It seems cheek on my part, since I saw so very little of you. I can tell you I was pretty jealous of Hubert; absurd as it may sound.

It was thinking of you at the last made me hate going away, but I hadn't the nerve to say so. Then, when we knew that the concession was all right, I knew what I had to do, what I couldn't help doing. That was to come back to you. Of course I am trying to prepare myself for the worst, and if you have to turn me down, I promise not to worry you again or obtrude myself more than I can help.

But, my dear, I hope it won't come to that. I hated myself for funking asking you for a photograph. I would have given my head for one. My mind helped me by making one of you. It is you, and it never goes out of my mind. I can see you there as clearly as if you were before me.

That night when we had the rumpus with the leopard, I did not know if I would come out of it at all well. But I knew I couldn't get knocked out before I had seen you again. That sounds foolish, but it

184

was the idea I had. Now you know what I feel about you, Patricia, and what you mean to me. If you could let me know in some way— I don't know what way—that I have a chance, I'll he everlastingly grateful. I don't know that I could hear to face you without knowing, but if it can't be, I would try to live the feeling down.

Patricia smiled at the letter, and then she laughed at the ending, for Peter had signed himself:

Yours sincerely,
   Peter Carey.

But it was a laugh that would not have embarrassed a lover—a happy, tender little laugh.

"You poor old thing!" she said to herself. "You poor darling Peter!"

It was so like him, in his love and his diffidence, his deep feeling, and his modest reluctance to imagine that she could really look at him as he looked at her. And at the end that ceremonial term "yours sincerely"! He was taking no premature advantages, doing his best instead to give her an easy way out, if she found herself unable to return his passion.

How different it would have been with the easy, sophisticated Hubert. He would have made love like an expert, but the love-making of an expert has no savour save for a moment. The after-taste of it is bitter and barren.

All that day Patricia went about shining. Miss Froud at the office noticed it, and wondered. Even Inspector Hoe when he turned up unexpectedly with a folded newspaper in his hand, made a mental note that Miss Repton must have had a bit of luck.

"She was smiling like a basket of chips," he said to his wife when he got home that night. "I wonder if that young fellow knows his luck?"

Patricia made him sit down, and glanced at his folded newspaper with an observant eye.

"Did you come to show me something?"

He opened out the *Daily Mail* and nodded. "Yes, miss. It seems these people got hold of news of the tragedy, and there is a par about it. I wondered if it meant Mr Carey had smelt a rat."

Patricia's eyes followed his pointing finger and read an account cabled from Mombasa.

Our East African correspondent today informs us that the Carey-Townard safari, which recently struck up into the interior in search of big game, is returning after a terrible tragedy which has cast a gloom over the district.

It appears that a leopard got into their camp one night, and terribly mauled Mr Townard, who was acting as professional hunter to the party. He had, it seems, snatched up Mr Carey's heavy rifle in the dark, and rushed to the aid of Mrs Gores, another member of the party, into whose tent the leopard had crept.

Two misfires occurred, and he was struck down before he could load again. He has since died of his wounds.

But here there is a notable coincidence, which has caused much comment. Mrs Gores' husband, a mining engineer and surveyor of some eminence, was killed the year before last by a wounded buffalo, as the result of a similar misfire at a critical moment. The rifle used in both cases was the same, having been purchased by Mr Carey from Mrs Gores on the eve of the setting out of the expedition.

Mr Carey declares that he is going home to probe this matter to the bottom, though he is not yet sure if the rifle or ammunition was at fault.

Patricia drew a long breath when she had finished. "That last bit is a trifle exaggerated," she said. "In Mr Carey's letter to me he merely says he is going to bring the rifle home to the makers. I don't think he suspected foul play for a moment, though this might make people imagine that he did."

"I suppose he was rightly indignant about it, and the correspondent took that natural view," said Hoe. "Well, the plot fell through, and Trevor is dead, so I have no one I can put my hands on. I'm sorry, in a way, for I was just making a case of it."

Patricia laughed. "I can't sacrifice Mr Carey to make your case!"

"I was thinking of Trevor," he said laughing too. "If he had survived the mauling we should have had him. We cabled out just before we heard of his death. We could have had those cartridges examined, and if they were tampered with, we could have had him held on that until we worked up the evidence of his having killed Hanaper."

"You will drop it now?"

"Certainly, miss. We don't exist to drag up dead men for nothing. We are far too busy for that. Trevor is dead, and he died as Townard. Let him be buried as Townard."

"I think you are right," she said.

Inspector Hoe looked like a man who could have said more. "Will you tell Mr Carey what you think of it when he comes back, miss?"

She shook her head. She knew she would be too happy and far too much engaged when Peter came home to worry about what might have been. "I don't think so. What good could it do?"

Inspector Hoe looked about him doubtfully, then he studied Patricia for a few minutes.

She was looking at the newspaper account again, and did not notice that he was watching her so closely.

When she glanced up once more he shook his head slowly.

"Can you keep a secret, miss?"

"If I promise to, yes," she replied, smiling.

"I am sure of it," said Hoe, "and as a good deal of work I did never came to the ears of my superiors, I was so afraid of making a mistake, no one but you and I will know of it now."

"You are very mysterious," she said. "I have often wondered, though, why you told me so much. It isn't usual for you gentlemen at Scotland Yard to be so communicative, is it?"

He smiled. "No, it isn't, and that's a fact. If it had just been Hanaper's murder, though you did put me on the right line about that, you wouldn't have heard much. But it was something much nearer you."

She stared. "Nearer me?"

"In one sense, at your elbow on more than one occasion. You knew one or two things I didn't."

Patricia had felt from the first that Hoe was a deep well who did not advertise his depth. His eyes were brooding again now.

"What do you mean?" she demanded.

He shrugged. "I wonder if you will think me not quite right in my head if I tell you the theory I formed some time ago. I began to wonder sometimes if I hadn't got a bit above myself with it. Yet I had a case worked up that I could hardly see a flaw in, and if I had been able to have Trevor arrested, he might have squealed."

"Squealed?"

"Turned informer, though I am not sure of that. He had the chance when he was ill out there, but didn't take it, and we know that he got Hanaper off in that confidence case by sticking to it that he had duped him as well as the Yankee."

Patricia nodded. "Oh, you mean that he might have confessed?"

"I mean that I believed, and I am still inclined to believe, that there was another man behind him. But he dies, and I can never get it confirmed."

Patricia was excited now. "But why another man? What could be the motive? You can't mean Hanaper, who is dead."

"I mean Mr Gage-Chipnell!" said Hoe. "That's who I mean, miss!"

CHAPTER 25 THE CASE FOR THE PROSECUTION

For a few minutes after Inspector Hoe had spoken, Patricia sat dumb and petrified with surprise and horror. Then her sense of the ludicrous came to her aid, and she laughed loud and long.

"It's utterly absurd," she cried, between gusts of laughter; "too preposterously funny!"

Hoe looked neither offended nor amazed by her way of taking his suggestion. He waited till her merriment had died down and she was wiping her eyes, before he spoke.

"Right, miss!" he said. "It does sound all that, and no one is better aware of it than I. But our job brings us into contact with every kind of odd thing that proves true in the end."

"But Mr Gage-Chipnell, Peter's cousin, who was very fond of him," she cried, her smile coming out again—"if you only knew him!"

"If either of us did," he said, "we'd know more than we do."

Patricia looked grave again. "Inspector, this is a very serious charge you have made, and I think an unfair one, if you are not prepared to justify it. I know you can't bring it out in public now, but you have told me, and I should prefer not to have such an idea on my mind if you cannot prove it to the hilt."

"That's fair," he remarked; "fair and proper, and I am going to tell you how I came to the conclusion and why. But we will

189

have to go back a bit, first back to Hanaper's trial, and later even further back than that."

"Very well. What was there in the trial you spoke of to justify your suspicions about Mr Gage-Chipnell?"

He set his fingers-tips together, and seemed to brood for a moment. Then he began.

"As you know, I found that Hanaper had been tried with Trevor, under the alias Williams, for tricking an American lawyer. To refresh my memory about the details of the case, I consulted our files. I found in the first place that both prisoners had been defended by counsel called Lossardle, instructed by a certain firm of solicitors. That was nothing in itself until I heard that Mr Gage-Chipnell was Mr Carey's cousin."

Patricia nodded. "I told you."

"Quite, miss. One of my colleagues knew the law firm, and he told me Mr Gage-Chipnell had been taken in as a junior partner within the last eighteen months."

"But that fact doesn't incriminate him?"

"No, miss. But let me get on. Mr Gage-Chipnell was at first in the firm's City office. The West-End one never took up criminal cases. It was a high-class family affair, but the other did all kinds of law business. I got a bit suspicious when I heard Mr Gage-Chipnell had seen Hanaper in your office, but I couldn't trace any interview between him and Hanaper prior to the confidence-trick trial, so I thought perhaps he would not have seen him before, and could not recognise him as Williams, for whom the firm had acted as well as Trevor."

"You mean that if he had seen Williams here, he would have recognised him?"

"Quite. But my enquiries told me he had had an interview with Trevor, while the managing clerk to the firm had taken over Hanaper's side. You see, the defences of both men were undertaken separately, as Trevor disclaimed any connection with Williams, and Williams posed as one of the tricked."

"Then how do you come to say that Mr Gage-Chipnell—" began Patricia, bit her lip, and added, "How stupid of me! Of course,

I see it now. Mr Gage-Chipnell had taken instructions from his client Trevor, so obviously must have known him."

"That's it. I had dropped Mr Gage-Chipnell out of the reckoning at first, but the moment you recognised Trevor as the man Townard, he came into the picture again. Then I remembered your telling me that Mr Carey had first seen your advertisement of the African business through his cousin showing it to him."

"So he did."

Hoe nodded. "All along I had been asking myself why Hanaper had taken that thing to you. He must have known that you were not a buyer but an agent, and the fact that you were a woman and inexperienced would not induce a buyer to take a pup. But if someone was anxious to get Mr Carey out to Africa, what was to prevent that someone from sending Hanaper to you with this proposition, and then drawing Mr Carey's attention to it?"

"Nothing but the lack of a motive."

"I'm coming to that, miss. So long as I didn't know who Townard really was, that motive was obscure. But your discovery threw a light on it at once. Mr Gage-Chipnell had seen Trevor and knew him. He recommends to his cousin a man he calls Townard as an experienced hunter for Mr Carey's African trip. That fact implicates him at once. What honest man would recommend a convicted scoundrel under a false name to a gentleman to whom he wished well?"

Patricia bit her lip. "You needn't labour that; I see it at once."

She saw several things then on which she had laid no stress before. She remembered how assiduous Hubert had been when she first met Peter Carey, how he had always been on hand to take her out in his car, or to monopolise her when Peter was about. But the moment Peter had gone, he had dropped his attentions to her, and she had hardly seen him at all.

Then she could not forget his anxiety when she had jokingly referred to joining the expedition as a chaperon for Peter and Mrs Gores, or his determined objection to Mrs Gores accompanying the safari.

It seemed clear enough that he suspected them both of matrimonial designs on his cousin, and had tried to enclose Peter in a ring fence until he could get him out of the country. No doubt, in the end, he had seen that Mrs Gores was too devoted to the memory of her late husband to be a danger, or realised that his continued intervention would be no good.

Hoe glanced at her sharply, and went on, "What you said put a few threads in my hands, but I was still rather at sea. Admitting that Mr Gage-Chipnell consorted with these rogues, and had got up a conspiracy with them to induce Mr Carey to go to Africa, I asked myself what the partner in a good firm of lawyers could gain by that. In other words, the real motive was to seek."

Patricia looked at him interestedly. This large, calm man had ideas. "You didn't suspect him of the murder of Hanaper?" she asked.

He smiled. "For a few hours I did! Hanaper dead, was one less witness to the conspiracy. But then I did not believe that he was clever enough with a gun to make that shot, or agile enough to do a cat-burglar stunt up a pipe. Hanaper's share of the loot was the money he was to get out of Mr Carey, but I asked myself where Trevor alias Townard came in. He was going out into the wilds with Mr Carey, what was he getting out of it?"

"I wonder," said Patricia eagerly.

"Well, miss, when a question like that comes up, we professionals don't sit down to deduce, we just make enquiries. If we have reason to suspect a man, we want to know who he was, what led him to act wrong, and what are the state of his finances. And we begin at the beginning, which is the right end."

She nodded. "A long way, but probably sounder."

"The first thing that struck me, miss, as it may have struck you, was the fact that Mr Gage-Chipnell had the same name as his uncle, and Mr Carey hadn't. Also Mr Gage-Chipnell was the elder. Old country gentlemen like the uncle have a decided liking for having the name carried on in connection with the estates. You find some of them even making wills declaring that the heir must adopt the family name. So I said to myself, why is Mr Carey

192

the heir, and Mr Gage-Chipnell not? But, to know that, I had to get down to the spot, so I went to Chipnell, and took rooms in the village."

"Your holiday tour?"

He smiled. "No, that was another place. Chipnell is nothing, apart from the family at the Chase. All the people are either employés or pensioners of the family. I got to know there that Mr Gage-Chipnell, the one you know, lived at the Chase with his uncle a year or two before Mr Carey went there as a very small child. His uncle sent him to a good prep school, and then to a public school, and it was understood, though not given out, that he was his uncle's heir."

"Really?" cried Patricia.

"So I understood, miss. Now, from what I heard of the uncle, he was a rare old sportsman. He gave every one a fair chance, and even if he disliked people he did not expose them—he simply sent them about their business. And he was very keen not to have any smirch on the family name. I don't know what happened at that public school, and those few who knew locally kept their own counsel, but I do know that Mr Gage-Chipnell came back before his time was up. Whatever had happened, his uncle gave him another chance. Then another thing happened, I imagine, though still nothing was said openly. The old man sent Gage-Chipnell to London, and Mr Carey, the other nephew, was installed as favourite. Mr Gage-Chipnell did not go down to the place again while his uncle was alive."

"But surely Mr Carey must have known that his cousin had done something very unpleasant?" she asked doubtfully.

"I don't believe it. From what I heard of the old man he would not injure even the defaulting nephew by telling his cousin about him. He just cut him off, and there was an end of it."

"Cut him off without any money?"

"I imagine he must have bought Gage-Chipnell into the law firm, paid for the partnership, I mean."

"But that partnership must have brought in something?"

"A good deal, I imagine, miss. However, I had some of my

facts. Mr Gage-Chipnell's conduct, when younger, had been sufficiently bad to make his uncle disinherit him. I can't make out what he did at the school, or when he came home, but the uncle's action speaks for itself. My job when I got back to town was to have a look at the old man's will. He left everything to Peter Carey (the estate is not entailed), and he added that, if Peter thought fit, he might make some provision for his cousin Hubert Gage-Chipnell. Not a word of reproach for the latter, though, which was generous in the old man, I think."

"Then Hubert Gage-Chipnell was the next of kin?"

"Exactly, miss."

She stared straight before her. "Horrible!"

Inspector Hoe shrugged. "Well, I had a possible motive, but it had to be reinforced before I could go on safely. Women and horses take up most of a libertine's money, and I had enquiries made on both lines."

"I saw her once!" said Patricia, and then wished she had not said it.

"A high-stepper, miss," he said, nodding, "She put as much on her back in a year as he would make out of his job. Then he had a car and chauffeur, and—well, a second house to keep up—which looked like money going away all ends. I took up the other enquiry myself, and got in touch with some racing-men I know, and I heard that Gage-Chipnell had been a heavy bettor for years. He had come down badly that spring over the National, and did even worse this year on the Derby. One of my informants also said he was a regular visitor at a private gaming-place someone had set up near Regents Park."

"Who kept it?"

"A former pal of Trevor's, though not of Williams. I expect that is where this ugly job was started. Gage-Chipnell probably got behind in his settlements, (gave a stumer cheque, perhaps) though I can't be sure of that—and was up against it. Likely he met Trevor there, recognised him, and evolved this scheme with him."

"But why should he confide in a man whom he had known was

a rogue of that kind?"

"Well, miss, he must have made some break that gave him away to Trevor's pal, and they may have threatened him between them with exposure. That would make even more money necessary to clear him unless he could find a large sum."

"You are sure he was in debt?"

"I am sure he is up to the neck in it now! There is a lien on his other house and furniture, though he took that house in an assumed name, and I believe he is being heavily dunned."

She shook her head sadly. "What a terrible state of affairs! If this is true, it does explain it."

"Quite, miss. Now, we have another point. Mr Carey, according to you, is a very attractive young man. Until lately he stayed at the old place in the country, and hunted, and so on, like the old sportsman his uncle. But when he came to town, he was a very eligible match for anybody, and his cousin must have known it. If he got married, the fat was in the fire, from the cousin's point of view."

Hoe looked at her for a few moments attentively, and, as she did not reply, he went on. "Now, miss, I am going to ask you an odd sort of question, but if you don't care to answer it, you needn't.—Did it strike you that Gage-Chipnell was anxious his cousin should not marry?"

Patricia nodded. "Curious that you should ask that."

"But it's true?"

"Yes—I think so."

He did not pursue the subject. He knew that Peter had not been encouraged by his cousin to pursue at least one lady. Patricia's eyes were tell-tale as she looked at him.

"Of course, miss, if I had known all this about Trevor being Townard before Mr Carey went away, I should have warned you, and you could have told him. But I didn't know, and earlier on I had no idea that Mr Gores' death might have been the result of foul play of a kind.—It was just chance saved Mr Carey from getting what Gores got."

Patricia shivered a little, but said nothing. He went on:

"Once a man gets into the hands of a gang like the Trevor gang, he has to go the whole way with them, or pay up. He couldn't afford to pay up, so he made his plan. It needed two other men to carry it out, and Trevor, no doubt, brought Hanaper in. Hanaper had come back to this country with the papers he had stolen from Gores, but he couldn't be sure of disposing of them. The lawyer's plight suggested a way. Here was a wealthy young man who wanted to do a bit of pioneering in Africa. He was a man who knew nothing of business or concessions. It would be an easy matter to string him, and, even if he raised technical objections, there was his lawyer cousin to say the papers were quite in order."

"Wait a moment," said Patricia. "Hubert objected at first."

"Very likely—but he agreed after. He put in that objection so as to appear disinterested; a regular rogue's bluff."

Patricia's eyes narrowed. "Do you mean to suggest that he put it to Trevor in cold blood that his cousin should be put out of the way?"

Hoe shook his head. "There are more ways of killing a cat than choking it with cream, miss."

CHAPTER 26 NEWS

For a minute or two after Inspector Hoe had made that enigmatic remark, Patricia remained silent, her eyes cast down. Then she met his eyes steadily.

"Do you mind explaining that?"

"Well, miss, I don't suppose even murderers talk openly about murdering people; not many, anyway. Trevor was as cunning as a monkey. I expect he just said if Gage-Chipnell could get him out with Mr Carey, all would be well. I can imagine him saying that in the wilds all sorts of accidents did happen; people getting cut off from their guides and lost in the bush, or getting some fever and dying of it, or running up against a ferocious beast of some sort."

"Do you suppose he knew what had happened to Mr Gores?"

"You mean Gage-Chipnell? No; I don't suppose they told him that. That would be giving him a handle against them, while they only wanted to have him tied up. But he would know what they meant, without details, and he was desperate, presumably."

"It turns on that."

"It does. Now he is at Monte Carlo, miss, where the desperate gambler often goes for a final fling."

"I know that," said Patricia slowly. "I heard, he had been playing high," she looked at him again, and added, "But, really, why do you tell me all this? We can get no evidence against him, now that Hanaper and Townard are dead and the plot has failed."

Inspector Hoe smiled a little. "Well, miss, we never like to leave people without warning of trouble. Mr Carey is coming back. His cousin is in a worse plight than before. Presently it will be make and break with him. As things stand, he will not know that I suspect what he was up to, let alone you."

"You think he might make another attempt?"

"I don't know, but I thought it was my duty to warn you, and leave it to you to tell Mr Carey. If I had given that warning without anything to back it, something might happen."

"I wouldn't have believed you, of course."

"Likely not. But now you know, miss, and I am out of this job. We may take it for certain that Gage-Chipnell paid Trevor alias Townard to go with his cousin, and *he did not pay him for nothing!* That's the long and short of it."

Patricia looked worried. "I am more grateful to you than I can say, Inspector," she murmured. "It was more than good of you to take so much trouble. Of course, I know you hoped to arrest Trevor for the murder of Hanaper, but you did so much more."

"That's all right," said he, rising and holding out his hand. "You'll tell Mr Carey when he comes back?"

"I must," said she. "I don't like it, but I must."

"If he isn't convinced, turn him over to me, miss," remarked the Inspector.

When he had gone, Patricia sat for a long time thinking. Every moment she saw the thing more clearly; from Hanaper's diffident entry into her office, to the last tragedy, when Trevor faced the leopard with a rifle loaded with shells he himself had rendered innocuous. So the man had entered into judgment with himself.

But to tell Peter would be a different matter. He had believed Hubert devoted to him, a sort of helpful elder brother, fussy, but affectionate.

And Hubert, even in the toils of debt, was inexcusable, selfish; cruel, callous, still a menace if he found an opportunity. She must guard Peter against that, whatever happened.

Mrs Elphinstone telephoned to her before she closed the office, asking her to dine with them that evening. Patricia went. She felt that she did not care to be alone just then. She must have someone to talk to, someone who would take her mind from the horror of Inspector Hoe's narration.

The two old people were in high spirits that night, and insensibly, gradually, Patricia found herself more calm and cheerful. Peter was coming home, alive and well. They all talked about him. Neither of her friends spoke of Hubert just then, and she was grateful.

After dinner, Mrs Elphinstone asked her husband if he had brought the evening paper. Mr Elphinstone hadn't. The billiard handicap at his club was in its semi-final stage, and, either by good luck or good guidance, he had got to that glorious penultimate phase among the veterans.

"How could you expect him to think of news when he was among the heroes?" cried Patricia. "I wished you luck the other day, didn't I?"

"You certainly did, my dear," he said, beaming. "I have no hesitation in attributing my—er—progress to your encouragement."

"You have your glory, but I haven't even my evening-paper to look upon," said his wife, with a twinkle.

"I shall send out at once, my dear," he cried contritely.

"Nothing of the sort," said the old lady. "The news will be fresher in tomorrow's papers. Play us something, Pat.—But it must not be 'See the conquering hero comes'!"

Patricia played to them, and then left early. A late edition of the evenings papers seemed in hot demand as she came into Oxford Street.

A placard at the tube station caught her eye, and she stared at it, wondering. Then she went across, bought a copy, and suddenly felt cold.

On the front page was a heading that froze her blood. It had been repeated on the placard, but there she had seen no evidence to prove that the event was connected with friend or acquaintance. On the page itself it gave name and hour.

"Suicide of a London Lawyer at Monte Carlo!"

That stark line told her all. She did not read any more until she had got home and was sitting in her little room.

It was Hubert Gage-Chipnell surely enough. Her eyes raced down the lines.

A terrible tragedy took place this morning in a villa near Monte Carlo. Mr Hubert Gage-Chipnell, a London solicitor, and partner in a well-known West-End firm, was the occupier. It was known that he had been indulging in very high play, and was said to have lost very large sums, but there is at the moment no proof that his death by his own hand was due to financial difficulties.

Yesterday evening he returned late from the rooms, and it is reported that he was in excellent health and spirits. About eleven o'clock this morning, he was sitting in the salon alone when a servant brought him the London papers. No one saw him again until twenty minutes past eleven, but at that time the sound of a firearm brought some of the household to his help.

To their surprise and horror they found him dead in his chair, with a six-chambered revolver lying across his knees. One chamber had been discharged. A surgeon was at once sought, but pronounced death to have been instantaneous. The sad affair has cast a gloom over the district.

Up to the time of writing, no further details have come to hand.

Patricia dropped the paper, and sat very still. She was shocked and horrified by the tragedy.

It was not so long since she had seen Hubert. Debonair, amusing, enjoying his world, he seemed the last man to think of destroying himself.

Would she have to tell Peter now what had really happened? It was hard to say. She knew, as surely as if the newspaper had explicitly stated the fact, that Hubert had seen that report from Mombasa, knew that Peter Carey was alive and well, realised that there was no escape now from the mountain of debt he had piled up about him.

Perhaps he had read more into it. The final paragraph might, to a guilty mind, suggest enquiry and condemnation. Suppose he imagined Trevor had confessed to his part in the scheme as he lay dying. The hint that Peter Carey was coming home to probe the matter to the bottom, though it was an exaggeration, would convey a menace to the man who had planned.

That night she hardly slept. She went over the affair step by step in her mind. She saw Hubert sitting in his chair in the villa, opening his newspaper, seeing there the ruin of his plan, at last facing the crash he had made inevitable.

Next morning she went to the offices of his firm. The partner who had received her before received her then. He was very white, and seemed worried, when she entered his office.

She talked to him of the tragedy for a few minutes, but he seemed to be thinking of something else.

"I am afraid he lost more than he could afford," she said.

The lawyer came out of his daze violently. "More than he had any right to lose," he snapped. "Such a thing has never happened in our firm before."

She stared at him. Surely no one thought that suicide of a partner was usual in any firm.

"I don't quite understand," she faltered.

He calmed down. "My dear Miss Repton, he went at my request to see a French client of ours at Aix. This gentleman was selling a vineyard in Burgundy. The sum of one hundred and ninety thousand francs was handed over to Mr Gage-Chipnell. We have heard this morning that not a franc of that sum reached our client."

Patricia gasped, but said nothing. The crash had been worse than she thought. The lawyer looked at her, and went on.

"You knew Mr Gage-Chipnell. I suppose you have no idea of the state of his finances?"

She shook her head. "I only met him through his cousin Mr Carey."

"You didn't suspect he was in debt?"

Patricia said nothing, but he saw that she knew.

"I quite understand your attitude," he said in an aggrieved voice. "We shall have to stand this loss, I suppose."

Patricia found her voice. "I can't speak for Mr Carey, but I imagine he would like to pay that rather than have the matter canvassed. How much is it?"

"In English money, you mean? Oh, let me see, about one thousand five hundred and fifty-five pounds."

"Then please wait."

"Is Mr Carey on his way home?"

"Yes. I heard from him lately."

The lawyer reflected. "Of course. How stupid of me. Have you seen *The Times* this morning?"

"I haven't seen a paper yet."

He got up and brought that day's issue. "Here we are, Miss Repton. It is a most extraordinary coincidence that is described today. It appears that, just before his death, Mr Gage-Chipnell must have been reading an account of his cousin's African experiences.—Some incident having to do with a leopard which attacked a companion of his.—I did not go very carefully into the matter, but that struck me forcibly."

Patricia took the paper and read a passage he indicated. Hubert had a copy of the *Continental Daily Mail* beside his chair and had absently marked with a pencil the paragraph cabled from Mombasa.

"Purely a coincidence, of course," said the lawyer, as she looked up again. "Well, Miss Repton, I am inclined to do as you say. The dead man's uncle was a man for whom I had the greatest respect. I should be sorry to have any slur on the family name. We shall await communication from Mr Carey when he returns."

Patricia got up and thanked him. He shook his head sadly.

"I would have given a great deal to have prevented this," he said. "But Mr Gage-Chipnell never confided his difficulties to me. Had he done so, I might have suggested some means of—er— liquidating them."

Patricia went on to her office. Miss Froud was full of the tragedy. She remembered seeing Mr Gage-Chipnell, and had thought him rather romantic-looking.

Patricia went hurriedly into her own office and shut the door. She was beginning to get over the shock of the news. From the shock emerged a new relief. She could not forget what Hubert had tried to do. The very tragedy was a proof that Hubert had been hopeful to the last that his callous plan might succeed. Busy with his gaming, he had known nothing of the progress of events in Africa.

He had sent messages to his office from various places, but most of the time he had been at Monte Carlo in his villa. Her letters, her wire even, must have failed to reach him.

The Mombasa cable had shown him the wreck of his plans: Trevor dead, Peter alive and coming home to make enquiries. "A guilty conscience needs no accuser," says the old proverb, and Hubert had chosen the one way out.

CHAPTER 27 BY WIRELESS

Crashes like Hubert's have short reverberations. For a week there was talk of his debts, and his death. Creditors mourned over big bills and exigent assets. The lease of his flat was sold, the furniture, the house he had bought elsewhere. The lady of the Riviera villa did not stay to explain her part in the extravagance but fled with the jewels Hubert had given her.

In all, a sum of nine thousand pounds was made up to meet claims in excess of twenty thousand.

Then the thing was swamped by other and more stirring things. An earthquake in China undermined it; a divorce in high circles absorbed attention.

Patricia was excited now. Hubert became a pale shadow in her mind, for Peter was on the sea, and every day brought him nearer. He had begged her to let him know if he had a chance. She read that letter of his over and over again.

Of course he had a chance, but how was she to let him know it? She felt unaccountably diffident about that, and feeling as she did was more inclined to excuse what he had called his 'cowardice.' Poor old Peter! Would he ever understand that the shyness that embarrassed him might also embarrass Pat?

"Your young man will soon be home," Mrs Elphinstone told her one day. "I wonder if he has heard about his cousin?"

"How could he?" said Patricia.

"I thought these liners had news by wireless," said the old lady.

"I never thought of that," said Patricia.

"Don't blush, my dear!" cried Mrs Elphinstone, looking at her amusedly. "He certainly can't hear me calling him 'your young man' by wireless. We haven't got to that stage yet."

"That's a mercy!" replied Patricia.

"Isn't it? Are you going to meet him?"

"I? Good gracious, no! What would he think of me?"

"That depends on what he thinks of you now, my dear," was the answer.

Patricia went home thinking of it. Of course, there would be wireless on the ship, and a message would reach Peter before he came to port. He had asked her for a sign. Ought she to give him one?

She answered the question that evening by sitting down and covering several sheets of notepaper with trial messages. Then she tore them up and went to bed uncertain.

The next morning she went to the wireless cable office, and achieved in a moment what hours had failed to do.

Her message was as brief as it well could be, but she thought Peter would understand it.

"All Well. Patricia."

Peter would be home in a few days. She went to the office, gave Miss Froud a week's holiday, and visited an agent, into whose hands she put the sale of her lease and office furniture.

It was possible that Peter had not heard of Hubert's death. Not every item of news was received aboard ship, except, it might be, on the luxurious American liners. Patricia hoped not. It would cloud Peter's home-coming, and if he did not know she need not tell him at once.

Of course he would come straight on to the flat. She must have everything nice for him. Strange at this moment how weak and funny she felt thinking about it. She was not at all like a composed person who had taken a degree with honours in one of the direst of subjects. She felt womanish and small, and a little afraid.

And Peter would not help her in that. He would be afraid

himself, and so horribly self-depreciatory that he would hardly get on at all.

"And I can't propose to him," she told herself, laughing. "I shall feel absolutely silly."

Then came the day before his arrival, and if he trembled on his ship, she trembled ashore. It was absurd that in this age of wireless, of short skirts, lip-stick, jazz, and other hardening inventions emotions should still be so emotional. The farcical novel might declare that proposals were mere fables in slang, and barer than ever, but no legislation had set a brake on the pace of the heart, and Cupid might still be brought up in court charged with dangerous driving.

And suddenly Patricia knew that she preferred to be as she was, and love as it was; not commonplace and prosaic, but romantic and sentimental. What is the good of fires if no one gets burned?

Peter ought to arrive at twelve o'clock next day. By one, she might see him, if he came to Tilbury. She looked up the time-tables and put the hour at half past one.

She slept soundly that night, and did not dream of Peter. But that did not matter, for he was coming.

At two he had not arrived. By that time she was as restless as a cat. At a quarter past, she sat looking out of a window into the street. Not a sign. She had forgotten the tides perhaps. Or did they make no difference?—It was a question.

She looked in a mirror, and discovered that she was looking a perfect fright. She went to her bedroom, but was still dissatisfied when the bell rang.

What would Peter think if he knew she had been such an ass about it all? But there was no time to answer that question. She ran out of the room, slowed, and walked very sedately to the door to let him in.

But when she saw Peter's shy smile, and felt his hands tremble in hers, her courage came back with a rush.

"Glad to see you again, Peter," she said. "Come in! I expected you an hour ago."

"I got your message—Patricia," he said, as he followed her into her little sitting-room. "But I went to your office.—I found it closed up."

Patricia faced him, smiling. "I closed it, Peter, because, you see, I am giving up business."

THE END

Made in United States
North Haven, CT
14 November 2024

60268034R00126